FIGHTIN' WORDS!

Out of the corner of his eyes, Buck saw Matt get slammed into the wall, and he figured his brother was out of this fight.

One of the cowboys laughed at him. "Looks like you're all alone, sonny," he said.

Buck sneered at him. "That ain't so bad, I reckon, if all I'm facin' is three fallin'-down drunks like you and those other two oafs."

"You talk mighty big for a boy about to get his butt stomped into the dirt," the first said easily.

"Oh," Buck said, "you want to fight? Hell, I thought you were sent by the town quiltin' society come to flap your gums till I fell down dead."

Also in THE RAMSEYS series

**THE RAMSEYS
RAMSEY'S LUCK
MATT RAMSEY
BLOOD MONEY
RAMSEY'S GOLD
DEATH TRAIL
RAMSEY'S BADGE
THE DEADLY STRANGER
COMANCHE**

BAD BLOOD
WILL McLENNAN

JOVE BOOKS, NEW YORK

BAD BLOOD

A Jove Book/published by arrangement with
the author

PRINTING HISTORY
Jove edition/January 1991

All rights reserved.
Copyright © 1991 by Jove Publications, Inc.
This book may not be reproduced in whole or in part,
by mimeograph or any other means, without permission.
For information address: The Berkley Publishing Group,
200 Madison Avenue, New York, New York 10016.

ISBN: 0-515-10493-0

Jove Books are published by The Berkley Publishing Group,
200 Madison Avenue, New York, New York 10016.
The name "JOVE" and the "J" logo
are trademarks belonging to Jove Publications, Inc.

PRINTED IN THE UNITED STATES OF AMERICA

10 9 8 7 6 5 4 3 2 1

BAD BLOOD

CHAPTER

★ 1 ★

Buck Ramsey didn't know what woke him. It was not so much a noise as it was a sensation; a feeling that something was not right. He rolled to his left and reached out, finding reassurance when his hand fell on the familiar, comforting Winchester.

"Matt," he whispered to the back of the snoring figure next to him. There was no response. "Matt!" he hissed with more urgency. Still there was no response; only a grumbled snuffling of air and a growled shifting back into sleep.

"Damn," Buck muttered, annoyed and a little nervous. Something was out there, and he was not happy about that. But what really bothered him was that Matt had not been himself since he'd been shot in a battle with Comanches two months before. Big Matt Ramsey had come close to dying then, but Buck—who had been escorting Miss Eula Mae McFarrin and her family north— had found his brother. Despite harassment and a running battle with the Comanches, Buck had managed to get to the rough town of Justice up in the Indian Nations, where Matt could get some care from a doctor.

Justice was a hellhole of a town, full of outlaws, cutthroats, and the dregs of humanity. Buck and Matt had left as soon as Eula Mae and her family were safely in the hands of her father and his men. The physician had warned the two Ramseys against it, saying that Matt was not ready for hard travel. But the Ramseys had ignored him and rode out, traveling as quickly as Matt's wound would allow, which was a plodding pace compared with their usual standards. Out of Justice more than a week now, they had camped for the night on a creek off the Wichita River.

Buck sat up quietly and began pulling on his boots as silently as he could. He heard a noise—clear, though soft—and Matt's big, midnight-black mustang nickered nervously. Something was disturbing the horses. It was, Buck figured, what had awoken him. And he was nervous, since it seemed someone was with their horses. And, since they were in Comanche territory, he worried that his old nemeses were back.

Buck finished with his boots, grabbed his rifle, and rolled out of the blankets. For a moment he pondered shaking Matt to wake him but decided against it. If his brother had not heard his whispers, he would probably wake loudly if shaken. Buck headed silently toward the horses in the thick shadows of the scrub oaks.

Matt awoke at Buck's initial call. He opened his eyes but did not acknowledge his brother. He was full of inner rage and self-loathing. He was angry at himself for not having heard whatever it was that had alerted Buck.

Just after Buck's initial hiss of warning, Matt had heard a soft noise, and he knew someone was trying to steal the horses. Damn, he thought, his anger growing to new heights. Not since his first days in the War of Secession had he felt so inadequate, so useless. He was usually the one who was first up and moving, on instinct for those first few moments before consciousness took over.

But since that Comanche raid, when he was wounded in the chest and his two wrangler friends died, he was not himself. He knew it, and his anger at himself percolated constantly just below the surface as he wallowed in self-disgust.

He had thought the worst of the wound's effects would be gone by now, but still they lingered, affecting his mind and soul as much as his body. His reflexes were slow, his normal alertness dulled, his instincts diminished. He had thought that being on the trail, where he would have to fend for himself at least somewhat, would help him. He knew from experience that there would be plenty of pain and that he would be weak and listless. He had been prepared for that and able to cope. But he was not prepared for the sluggishness of spirit that had infected him.

Matt knew he'd been a poor traveling companion for Buck, but there seemed to be nothing he could do to change that. Matt regretted being such a disappointment for Buck during their short journey from Justice. That made him all the more angry at himself.

Buck stalked off and Matt sighed, partly in relief, partly in the knowledge that he would have to help Buck despite his inadequacies. He threw off his blankets and slipped his boots on. Fighting off the cloying fog of tiredness and despair, he stood up, feeling the night's moist coolness on his face. Checking his big Colt .44, he stepped off into the darkness.

He heard the stealthy scrape of cloth on a tree branch and knew instinctively that it was not Buck, so he angled toward it. A figure darker than the surrounding darkness moved, the shifting blot of black catching Matt's attention. He moved up, wary. The feelings of inadequacy rose up inside him, threatening to burst out in a scream. The sensation, not the situation, frightened him. Usually his self-assurance and confidence were strong enough to overcome any fear he might have. But now he was not so certain of himself.

Matt jumped at the dark figure. As he tackled the form, he knew from the odor that he had latched onto an Indian. He only hoped there was not a passel of them. The Indian struggled mightily, and Matt began to worry that he might not have the strength to handle the would-be horse thief. But he'd be damned if he would call on his little brother for help. He'd rather die, he decided.

Buck had circled the fire, making sure to keep out of the pale orange puddle of light cast by the fading embers. He moved with quiet self-confidence, despite the rapidly blossoming worry in his belly. He was afraid that Indians were trying to steal the horses. Since he and Matt were nominally in Comanche country, he figured—maybe *feared* was the right word—the thieves were Comanches. And he had seen far more of those fierce warriors on the journey to Justice than he ever desired. He wanted no more truck with Comanches.

A dull shaft of light shimmered downward from the pale quarter moon, easing the shadows a little. He saw an ill-defined figure standing next to Matt's midnight mustang. The only thing Buck could tell about the figure was that it was an Indian.

The Indian—whom Buck, with more than a little relief, did not think was a Comanche—looked about ready to leap onto the horse. Buck set his Winchester down against a hackberry bush and ran. He slammed shoulder first into the Indian, sparking a vapid yelp of surprise.

The Indian fought back weakly, and Buck had no trouble subduing him. Finally settling himself on the enemy's chest, Buck yanked out his Colt. He cocked it and stuffed the muzzle up against the underside of the Indian's nose.

"I got no real desire to kill you, Injin," Buck said, his breath short. "But I ain't against such an idea either. Now ease off your fightin'."

The Indian struggled for a few more moments before resting, limp and wheezing.

It was so dark that Buck could tell nothing about the Indian, except knowing from touch that the Indian wore white man's clothing and had long hair.

"I'm gonna stand up," Buck said. "But you try anything and I'll plug you right where you stand. Understand?" He hoped the Indian understood English. He thought he saw the featureless face nod once, so he got up, still holding the pistol level. Buck's fear had lessened considerably. He knew this was no Comanche, and he figured there was only one other Indian around. Buck took the Indian's pistol from the worn holster and jammed it into his belt. He also relieved the subdued enemy of his Arkansas toothpick.

Buck heard a noise from several yards to his right, and he jerked in that direction, almost firing his Navy Colt by accident. The sounds of a struggle came from that direction, including several muffled grunts from his brother. He breathed in relief. Matt would handle whoever was out there; Buck had no fear of that. He moved around the warrior. "March," he said, prodding the Indian in the back with the Colt.

The Indian walked toward the camp, with Buck behind him, his pistol ready. "Sit," Buck ordered when they were at the fire ring. The Indian did so. Buck quickly grabbed a rope from where it hung on the pommel of his saddle and he tied the Indian up. He swiftly tossed some wood on the embers and knelt to fan the fire with his hat. Flames suddenly burst forth and licked greedily at the fuel.

Buck stood up, sweating from the sudden heat of the fire. He choked on the smoke, and his eyes watered. When his eyes cleared, he looked at the Indian. "Well, hell!" he muttered. It was no wonder he had had little trouble subduing the Indian. The warrior, Buck saw, was at least seventy years old.

The old Indian seemed positively ancient, with wrinkles coursing through his coppery face. Long, straggly hair of snowy white drifted down his back and along the sides of his face. His countenance seemed to sag with his years but retained an inherent pride. A great hooked beak of a nose thrust itself haughtily out from the center of the wizened face.

He looked forlorn, and the white man's clothing—woolen trousers and cotton shirt, as well as worn boots—added to the sad effect.

"What's somebody old as you—" Buck started, but he stopped as he noted Matt moving into camp, angrily shoving another Indian ahead of him. Matt looked to be in a towering rage.

Buck stopped talking partly because of Matt's arrival, partly because of his brother's evident anger, and partly because he was trying to stifle his laughter.

"Don't you dare, Buck," said Matt menacingly.

Buck looked ready to bust a gut as he tried to hold in the gale of laughter that was threatening to burst forth.

"And don't you say a goddamn word, neither," Matt added, with even more warning in his voice.

"I . . . won't . . ." Buck sputtered. But he was lying. Within moments he was laughing like a madman.

Matt scowled and shoved his prisoner forward by the shoulder. "Sit down, damn you," he snarled.

"That ain't no way to treat a lady, Matt," Buck said around his guffaws.

"Hell," Matt snapped, drawing the word out. "Just get some goddamn rope and tie her up."

The young Indian woman sat next to the old man, while Buck got more rope. As he began tying the girl up, Buck tried to get a good look at her without actually seeming to do so.

She was young—a little younger than Buck's seventeen years, he guessed. She was short and slender, with a long, graceful neck. She was pretty, too, he thought, with high, well-defined cheekbones, a sharp chin, long, thin nose, and large, dark, buckskin-soft brown eyes. Her long hair was as black as the night and hung loosely down her back, framing her cheeks. Though she smelled of sweat and grease under a muskiness, Buck was rather taken in by her.

Finished, Buck stood up and grinned. "Hope she didn't give you too much of a tussle, Matt," he said, laughter threatening to well up again. The jolliness was choked back by the combination of rage and hurt that had leaped into Matt's eyes. Buck was shocked at it.

"Just put on the goddamn pot and start some breakfast." Matt fought to control the lava of rage that bubbled inside. "Unless you want to . . . " He stumbled to a halt. Almost absent-mindedly, his right hand brushed the walnut grips of his pistol.

Buck stood for a few moments, stunned that his brother would even think such a thing. Troubled, he headed toward their supplies. He grabbed the coffee pot and dumped in a handful of Arbuckle's coffee. Then he filled the pot with water from the creek. After setting it on the fire and turning back toward the small pile of supplies under the canvas tarp, Buck glanced surreptitiously at Matt. His older brother stood back a bit, arms folded on his big chest, a hard, dull look on his rough face.

Wonder what's eatin' at him, Buck thought as he squatted by the supplies. He grabbed what was needed and went to kneel at the fire. Still confused, he began slicing off chunks of bacon into a blackened frying pan. In a pot, he quickly mixed beans with water and fatback. Buck set the breakfast on the fire to cook. He wiped his knife and then his hands on an old piece of cloth and tossed it aside. He stoked the fire a little better and then rocked back on his heels to wait.

Dawn was breaking, spreading a dull, gray light through the thick, rising tendrils of morning fog. But it was considerably lighter than it had been only minutes ago. Buck wondered—and worried—about Matt, but he tried to keep from thinking on it. Such thoughts would do him no good.

Besides, the young Indian girl was a pleasurable distraction. Her attractiveness seemed to have increased with the growing light, though the hard set of her jaw diminished her beauty fractionally. She would, he decided, be quite pretty if she softened her face and cleaned herself some—and if she were dressed better. The ratty calico dress she wore was torn and tattered, and there were several gaping holes that showed a bit more female skin than Buck was accustomed to seeing. Her moccasins were pitted and barely serviceable.

The girl's face was dirty and scratched; her hair snarled and tangled; and a purplish bruise discolored her right cheek. Other bruises marked her legs, which were bared some as she sat haphazardly.

Despite all that, the girl retained a sense of defiance and anger, much as the old man remained proud and somehow regal, even though he looked worn and decrepit.

CHAPTER
★ 2 ★

Buck poured some coffee into a tin mug and carried it to his brother. The older Ramsey took it without a word. Stung by Matt's bitterness, Buck shrugged and went back to the fire. He poured some coffee for himself and drank it slowly, thankful for its warmth against the coolness of the morning. He was also aware of the four dark, angry eyes glaring at him.

Finally he set the mug down. "Food's ready, Matt," he said quietly. He did not expect an answer from his brother, and he was not disappointed.

Matt took the tin plate of beans and bacon Buck held out. He went back to a position out of the way and sat down, his back braced against his saddle. He ate silently, sullenly.

Buck filled his own plate and shoveled in the food, hardly tasting it. He was disturbed by his brother's actions and attitude. He had never seen Matt like this before. When he finished, he asked, "Reckon we ought to feed these two, Matt?"

"Why?" Matt growled, tossing the plate in Buck's direction. It skittered across the dirt and stones. "They ain't nothin' but horse thieves. And piss-poor ones at that."

"Hell, Matt, they're a girl and an old man."

"There ain't nothin' worse'n horse thieves, Buck. You've run enough mustangs with me to know that. The best they deserve is a hangin'." There was no give in his voice.

"Well, Matt," said Buck slowly, bracing himself, "I'm fixin' to feed 'em." He paused. "Whether you like it or not." He wasn't sure if his brother would try anything, but the way Matt had been acting of late, he was a bit worried about the possibility.

But Matt only shrugged and turned away.

Buck stood up and walked around the fire to the Indians. He knelt down between them. "I let you two loose to eat, you gonna cause me trouble?" he asked.

The girl was nearly as sullen as Matt, and she said nothing. But the old man said firmly, "No." He turned to the girl and said a few garbled-sounding words to her in what Buck guessed was their tongue. She seemed about ready to argue but then nodded curtly, sneering at Buck.

Buck grinned stupidly at her, not knowing what else to do. He untied both. He scooped some bacon and beans onto his plate and Matt's, after giving them only a cursory wiping. Then he handed the plates to the Indians and sat back, watching warily as they ate.

When the Indians had finished, Buck let each go into the bushes, one at a time, to take care of personal needs. He had been worried that either—though especially the girl—might try to run. But an implied threat against the old man was enough, Buck thought, to keep her in line.

Finally, Buck bound the Indians again and cleaned up after the meal. Matt had said nothing the whole time. He only sat leaning against his saddle, looking either pained or furious. When the cleaning was done, Buck squatted just outside the ring of heat from the fire and looked across the dying flames at the two dark faces. "Just who the hell are you? And what's brought you way out here tryin' to steal our horses?" he asked.

There was silence from the Indians, though the sounds of life carried on all around them: the chirping of cowbirds and grackles, the raucous squawk of a jay, the ripple of the creek water, the hum of insects. They were comforting, normal sounds that belied the tension that crackled in the small camp.

Finally the old man said, "I am John Long Ridge, last chief of Echota, home of the Cherokee people." There was no mistaking the pride in his quavery voice, despite the fear that lurked inside him. He waved an arm vaguely in the girl's direction. "This is my great-granddaughter, Grace Red Bird."

"Pleased to meet you," Buck said, just missing a note of sarcasm. His face hardened a little. "Now, what the hell are you doing here?"

Long Ridge's face twitched as a grin fought to come out. He composed himself and said simply, "Tryin' to steal your horses." He had a little accent.

Buck smiled despite his resolve not to. He nodded. "All right, Mr. Long Ridge. Why?"

"We needed 'em."

Buck shook his head. This was worse than having a tooth pulled by old Doc Brown back in New Liberty. "Why'd you need 'em?" He held up his hand before Long Ridge could say anything. "I reckon you'd best start from the beginnin'."

Long Ridge stared at him a few moments before nodding gravely. "Two moons ago, Red Bird was stolen from our village up on Sallisaw Creek in the Nations."

"By who?"

The Indian shrugged. "All the white men look the same to us," he said with a straight face.

"Bullshit," Buck snorted.

Long Ridge stared at Buck. The old Cherokee was scared, though he would not show it. But so many years of abuse at the hands of the hated white man had made him edgy around any pale-skinned people. Still, there was something about this young white man that gave such angry thoughts pause.

"Harlan Cross and his men," said Long Ridge quietly.

"Don't know of him."

"A bad *hombre*, that one," the Indian commented. "A mean bastard." He hesitated, then said quietly, "I take it you boys fought for the Confederacy?" He looked at Buck with a question in his dark eyes.

Buck shrugged, embarrassed. "Matt did," he said, jerking his head in his brother's direction. "And our brother Kyle. I was too young." Regret lay thickly in his voice.

Long Ridge almost smiled. "As I was too old. But many of the young men of my village were in sympathy with the Confederacy, and some went to fight."

"You believe in slavery?" Buck asked, surprised.

Long Ridge did smile this time, though just a little. "Do you?" He thought he could tell a great deal about this young man already. Long Ridge had been on this earth many winters now, and while his young warriors might no longer look up to him, he had built up more than a little knowledge about the ways of men.

"Well, no," Buck muttered, suddenly on the defensive. "We . . . I mean, Ma and Pa . . . well, Matt and Kyle . . ."

"You do not think slavery is right, eh? But since your state went to war you thought you should join them?"

"Well, not me—exactly me—but . . ." He grudgingly admitted to himself that John Long Ridge knew what he was talking about. "And you?"

"My people have suffered greatly at the hands of the white man," said Long Ridge, his face and voice bitter. "Especially the goddamn blue coats. When the gray coats came along and offered us a chance to fight those bastards—and maybe even have a chance of bein' on the winnin' side—we grabbed that opportunity. Without thinkin' a hell of a lot about it." He shrugged fatalistically.

"What's all that about?" Buck asked, wondering. He could see no reason why Long Ridge had gone off on this tangent, and he wondered what it had to do with why Long Ridge and Grace Red Bird were in the Ramseys' small camp, trying to steal their horses.

"Harlan Cross fought for the Cause, too. Or so he likes to tell folks." He paused. "Cross rode with Quantrill at the beginning, and then with Cap'n Anderson. If that wasn't bad enough, he started off on his own after a while, killin' his own kind as well as the goddamn Yankees." His voice faded.

Matt jerked himself upright and stalked off, leaving Buck wondering once again just what was sticking in his brother's craw. But Matt was in no mood to listen to these Indians complain about the hard lot life had given him. He had his own worries. To hell with them; and to hell with Buck, too, he thought viciously, ignoring the pang of guilt that flooded over him.

Matt had begun to think he was less than a man lately. Certainly less than what he had been. And all because of one damned Comanche arrow. Actually, he had taken two arrows and a bullet, but only the one really counted. It cast an ugly pall over his life, and he was in no mood to deal with anyone else's troubles. He was in no humor to explain it—or even try—to Buck, who Matt knew was going *loco* with wondering. But no matter, Matt thought.

Buck stared at Long Ridge and Red Bird, wondering about them even more than he was wondering about Matt. "So, how'd this Harlan Cross come to take Miss . . . Red Bird?" he asked.

"My people were a proud people once," Long Ridge said, wistfulness making his voice heavy. "Before . . ." Tears leaked from his eyes, but Long Ridge did not care, and Buck did not think any the less of the old Cherokee. Nor did he think

Long Ridge was false in his sorrow, trying to trade on his sympathies.

Long Ridge shook off some of the gloom, which was replaced with the pain of loss. "But now we are weak, ineffectual. Our warriors ain't men any more. They are . . ." Long Ridge slapped his mouth shut and sat there, breathing harshly through his prominent nose while trying to collect himself.

Buck waited quietly. He did not mind the wait, not when there was Miss Grace Red Bird sitting across from him, looking as fine as she did, even with the anger and dirt and pain marring her normal beauty. This young Cherokee woman was damn near enough to make him forget Miss Eula Mae McFarrin, he thought.

He closed his eyes a moment, trying to conjure up a picture of Eula Mae. It was not that difficult when Grace Red Bird was not swimming in his vision. Eula Mae was about the same height as Red Bird and built much along the same lines. But there was a softness of face about Eula Mae, a warmth and even tenderness about the young white woman that this Cherokee would never be able to match.

A deepening sadness began to fall over his shoulders and seep over him. Then Long Ridge's voice broke into his pleasurably painful thoughts. He opened his eyes, sighing at the same time, trying to bring himself back to reality.

"Many men like Cross come to our village. Have been since the war ended. Most of 'em are runnin' from the law back in the states. We would trade 'em food and such for cash. They usually paid in greenbacks though, the cheap bastards." He almost smiled.

"He came for the first time two years ago. He's been back a few times since. Had I knowed the godless bastard was watchin' Grace, I'd have run him off a while back."

"Sure you would, Gramps," Red Bird sneered.

Buck flushed with anger at the look of distress that crossed the old man's face after his great-granddaughter's cutting words. "You ought to be more considerate of your elders, Miss Red Bird," Buck snapped.

Red Bird stared at Buck with flat eyes, though defiance contorted her face a little. She said nothing.

"It ain't important," Long Ridge said with a sigh. "She's probably right anyway." Long Ridge stopped and snorted, expelling nasal mucus. He shrugged up his left shoulder as best he could to be able to wipe the residue off on the already soiled cotton shirt.

"Well, shoot, he and his men come up to the village a couple months ago. They'd just pulled some kind of job over in Missouri and were on the run again. Must've been a good job, too," he admitted with a hint of grudging admiration, "since they were flush with cash. Bought some whiskey off a moonshiner upriver a ways and brung it down to the village."

Long Ridge's hurt gradually shifted to anger. "The boys up to the village had a hell of a spree once Cross and his pals brought out that forty-rod. Damn no good . . ."

He spit, his distaste for the debilitating behavior of his people nearly choking him. Their lack of moral fiber, their abandonment of all their social and cultural strengths sickened him.

"Once the spree was over, they rode off, headin' for Texas."

"And they took Red Bird," Buck said. It was not a question.

"Yes," Long Ridge muttered, discomfited again by the troubles life had thrown at him.

"Yes," Red Bird said obstinately, almost challenging Buck to say something about it.

Buck was still young, but he had seen much of the seamier side of life already, and he knew most often when keeping his mouth shut was wise. This was one of those times, he decided.

"Want to hear what happened to me while they had me?" Red Bird asked, disappointed at not having gotten more of a reaction out of Buck.

"Only if you feel like tellin' it," he said quietly. He had a pretty good idea why Red Bird had been taken; and he had an even better idea of just what those men had done to her. He could not, however, understand how men could do such a thing, or think it pleasurable.

"They all had me," Red Bird hissed, trying to shock Buck now, to shake him out of his seeming indifference. "Every one of 'em. There was nine of 'em, and the others that rode in and only stayed a little bit. And they took me every chance they got."

Buck looked down at the ground. He felt sorry for Red Bird, knowing she must be retching inside with self-disgust. That's why she was so defiant, he guessed; it was the only way she could hold her head up and look a man, any man, in the face.

"They took me every which way they could think of, and—"

"Enough, Granddaughter," Long Ridge said angrily. He did not like listening to this any more than Buck did. But he could respond and get away with it.

Red Bird fell silent, but she was angry, her faced diffused with the rage.

Buck sat and waited, letting the insects hum their way through the camp, listening to the birds chirping. After a while, he asked, "And how did you both get here?"

CHAPTER
★ 3 ★

John Long Ridge stood before the small assembly of men. He experienced a flood of memories, of a time more than forty years before. His people were still living in the East then, amid the piney ridges, peaks, gullies, and hollows of the Blue Ridge Mountains.

He had been a man in his twenties then, full of fire and hot blood; a warrior with a stout heart; a hunter without peer among his people. Then he was known simply as Long Ridge, and he was a chief despite his age. He was well-respected and looked up to by all the villages. By his people's standards—and even by those of the white man—Long Ridge was a wealthy man. He owned land and his farms were productive. He owned cattle and horses and pigs. And slaves. John Long Ridge had owned slaves then and saw nothing wrong with it. He had come over the years, since the Long Walk, to realize that slavery was not a good thing, that the owning of other human beings was an aberration of human nature.

But it had taken that Long Walk, in which thousands of his people died on the trail, and almost forty years of oppression to teach him such a thing.

But back then, when he would stand before his people, he was listened to. He could call for his warriors to go to war against other Indian peoples or against the steadily, inexorably increasing horde of white men that flooded into their land. And always he had been heeded. It had created a swell of pride—and yes, he would concede only to himself, arrogance, too—in him each time.

But the white men kept coming, hungering more and more for Cherokee land. And when gold was found in Cherokee land, the die was cast. Long Ridge saw that the Cherokees could not hold off the encroachment of the pale-faced ones, but he argued against giving up any of their land. He advocated war. He knew their land would be taken, but he argued frequently and harshly that the Cherokees should make the white man pay—in blood—for the land, rather than just signing some papers that gave their land away.

His view held sway for some time, and his people won small victories against the white gold seekers and the settlers. But the whites fought back, burning Cherokee villages, trampling their fields, killing livestock. Men, women, and children were slain, and the tide began to turn against the Cherokees.

Long Ridge was heeded far less then, and his people began to talk more of signing papers to cede their land. At least, many of the chiefs argued, the people would get something for their land then. If they continued to fight, they would be driven off their land and have nothing.

Long Ridge would not accept such a thing, and he argued forcefully that the white man had lied so often that speaking with a forked tongue was the only speech the white man knew any more. And he told his people that the whites would steal their land no matter what was promised. "It is better to fight for our land; to make the pale-faced ones take it by force and drive us out."

But soon the Great White Father far off in Washington decided that Cherokee land must be opened to white settlement and that the Cherokees would be given land out in the West, beyond the great Mississippi River, land the Cherokees could keep for all time.

The Cherokees acquiesced, despite the forceful arguments of Long Ridge and others like him. They had seen the Choctaws and Creeks marched out before them. They fought in courts, but even their victory there had done them no good. The decision was made, and the blue coats came when the cold had settled over the land. The Cherokees were herded together—along with the Creeks and Choctaws and others—like sheep and then driven slowly westward as the snow began to fall.

Long Ridge was pained whenever he thought about it. The old ones—who held the past, the language, the culture of the

Cherokee people—and the youngest ones—who held the future of the Cherokees—suffered the most. They died by the score as the pitiful exodus wound across hill and valley, across stream and river, through forest and across glade.

Until they had reached the rolling hills and desolation of the land the whites called Indian Territory. But the suffering of the Cherokee people did not end there, and over the next forty years, it ground them down, until even hard-core warriors like Long Ridge were worn and beaten.

But when he stood before his people on this occasion, just after Grace Red Bird had been taken, he remembered not the travails of the Trail of Tears or of its aftermath but the early days, when he was strong and proud.

"We have lost many of the people to the white man over the years," he said, his voice powerful and certain, though he had not called on it in many years for such a purpose. "Now another is gone." He paused. "But this is one of the people we might get back. I call on you, as warriors, as Cherokees, to go with me to bring her back."

His words were met by a dull, threatening silence. The people of Long Ridge's village had no spirit left.

"Are you not men?" he roared at the warriors. Most of the men—the younger ones never having really been warriors, the older ones living on memories—mumbled and looked at their feet. They would not face Long Ridge, who wanted more from them than they could give.

"Will you let Red Bird be abused by those evil men and not see that justice is brought to them? Are you such people that you have lost that which makes you men?" Long Ridge's rage soared toward the heavens, clouding the skies above them.

But neither his words nor his fury created any reaction other than indifference in the men. And the few women watching from nearby did not add their pleas to Long Ridge's, as the old chief had hoped they might.

"You are women," Long Ridge sneered at the warriors, hoping to shame them. "Less than women. Meek little groundhogs who dig holes in the ground and hide when danger is near. You are not worthy of being called Cherokees!"

He stood muttering imprecations against his weak-willed people. "Then I will save Red Bird. Alone! I will show you how a Cherokee should react when one of his people is stolen out from him!"

Long Ridge turned and stomped away, anger burning in his veins like lead melted down for shot, thick and heavy. Through the defeats back in the Cherokees' eastern homeland, through the Long Walk, in which two of his sons and a daughter perished, through all the oppression and humiliation afterward, he had never felt so shamed as he did now. He was disgusted with his people, humiliated beyond belief that they would sit there and do nothing.

His own wife looked at him proudly when he entered their log home. She came to him and rested her hands on his biceps. Long Ridge fought back the surging tide of rage within him and smiled down at Mavis Light Hair. He saw there not the aged, wrinkled, toothless, stooped old woman she was, but rather the beautiful, brown-haired young woman he had taken as his wife almost fifty years before, the daughter of Chief John Ross.

"You do not think me a foolish old man?" he asked.

"No." The white-haired head shook slowly. "What you are doing is right, my husband. The others"—she turned her head and spat in disgust—"are not men. They are . . ."

But Long Ridge was not listening any longer. "Saddle our horse," he ordered, finding in himself a wellspring of old dignity and courage. "I will gather my weapons."

Light Hair nodded and walked unsteadily out of their decrepit home. Once she had had a fine house, with wood floors. People—slaves she and Long Ridge owned—waited on her. But those days were long, long past, and she thought of them seldom. She hurried to the small corral in back of their home and called softly to the plodding old workhorse, the only one they owned. She found their ragged saddle blanket and tossed it on the horse's back. Then she struggled to get the worn saddle up onto the animal.

She was weak and shaking by the time she had accomplished this, and she had to take some moments to gather her strength back and get the bit and bridle in place. She led the horse to the front of the house and tied it. Inside, she told her husband shamefully, "You will have to tighten the saddle. I am too weak to do so properly." Bile rose up in her throat. Aging was hard on her, though she had lived far longer than most women of her people did.

Long Ridge nodded, knowing of her embarrassment. He had felt it himself far too many times in the past twenty-some years. His muscles no longer obeyed as he wished them to; his bones ached and made odd creaking noises when he used them; his teeth were falling out; and his eyesight was dimming. And because of those growing infirmities, he had become, over the decades, much like the others of his tribe—weak, ineffectual, spiritless.

But now he felt a new man. Grace Red Bird was his favorite of the few great-grandchildren he had. Her kidnapping by Harlan Cross and his fellow outlaws was too much for Long Ridge to accept. He would find her and rescue her. It was, he had decided, his last chance to do something important and even noble. He knew his limitations, but he would do what he could within them. He would bring Red Bird back—or he would die in the trying.

He stepped outside and stopped, hoping the others would be watching. He was dressed in a cotton shirt and heavy woolen pants; worn boots, hastily dusted off, covered his feet; a stovetop hat, into which he had stuck two turkey feathers, covered his head; a long, black, split-tail coat, the best he had, completed his attire.

He carried an old .54-caliber Starr carbine in his hand and a .36-caliber Texas Dance revolver in a holster at his right hip. On his belt were two hard-leather cartridge boxes, one to carry the linen cartridges for the short rifle, the other holding the pistol's paper cartridges. He also carried an Arkansas toothpick in a hard leather sheath.

Only a few people watched blatantly, but Long Ridge knew others were watching from inside their homes. He puffed his old chest out as much as he could. Setting the carbine down, he tightened the saddle, willing himself not to show the effort it took. He was left wheezing. He stuck the carbine in an old scabbard, made of poor buckskin.

Hauling himself into the saddle—while keeping a blank face and a straight back—was difficult, but he managed. He rode out slowly, sneering at his people, to let them know of his disgust with their ways. But as soon as he was beyond the outskirts of the village and fairly certain no one was following him, he slumped, leaning on the saddlehorn and gasping for breath.

John Long Ridge had never felt so useless and ineffectual. He thought of turning back and giving up this foolish quest. But he could not bear that shame, so he rode on, thinking he was going to die.

Over the next several weeks, Long Ridge thought frequently about giving up. He could stay out here a bit, hunting and relaxing, before riding back into the village. There he could tell the others that he had at least tried to do something for Red Bird.

But he knew he could not live with himself if he did such a thing. He would be better off just blowing his own brains out here, away from the village, and be done with it. So he pressed on.

He lost count of the days, though he did not care. Following the tracks of Harlan Cross and his men was easy at first, since the outlaws were not trying to cover their path. But after passing two towns and crossing a dozen streams, Long Ridge began to lose the trail. But still he went on, feeling younger and younger as he went.

The first week was the worst, as old muscles, long unused, complained. Pain and soreness afflicted him, worsened by frequent chilling rains.

But gradually he found himself having less trouble with some things, as his bones and muscles and ligaments responded to their new uses. He knew that he could never regain the vigor and strength of his youth; but at least now he didn't feel as if he were going to die any moment.

It took more than a month, but he finally caught up with Cross, who, with his men, had camped along a creek feeding the Salt Fork of the Brazos River. He held back, watching from a grassy ridge, as Cross's men rode across the gully a mile ahead. Long Ridge breathed a sigh of relief. He had not wanted to admit it, but he was not all that sure that Red Bird would still be alive. Such men as those who rode with Cross mostly used women and then cast them aside. But he could see her on a horse in the midst of the men. Long Ridge dismounted and lay on the grass. He slept.

When he awoke, it was dark. Long Ridge took a few moments to orient himself—and to curse himself silently for having slept for several hours. He quickly mounted and rode forward, painfully gnawing on some hardtack and the last of his jerky.

Three hours later, he heard sounds of men having a good time: drunken laughter, coarse language—and Long Ridge knew where that would lead to, especially with a young woman as beautiful as Red Bird in their midst—belching, and foolish chatter. He tied the horse and moved up cautiously on foot. Hiding behind a cottonwood, he peered at the small camp.

Seven men were there, all in various states of drunkenness. Long Ridge was disgusted. He could not see how any men—red or white—could let themselves fall under the spell of intoxicating beverages. It made men foolish and robbed them of their manhood.

While Long Ridge watched, one of the men stood up. As he walked, he unbuttoned his pants. The others laughed and hooted, pointing. With a leer, the man shoved Red Bird's dress up past her waist. The girl wore no undergarments, since they had been torn off by this band of savages long before. He threw himself on her. In moments he was done. He rebuttoned his pants and tried to swagger back to the fire but had a difficult time of it, as the liquor distorted his sense of balance. Throughout the ordeal, Red Bird had lain quietly, with a blank face.

Long Ridge felt sorry for Red Bird having to go through the sickening ritual—which the old Cherokee knew had to have been happening regularly since Red Bird was taken. But he was also proud of her. She withstood it stoically, biding her time, waiting, hoping someone would come after her. Long Ridge was proud of himself, too. Proud for having come in the first place; proud that he had not given up and turned back.

Now all he had to do was set her free.

CHAPTER
★ 4 ★

John Long Ridge found reserves of patience he had not known he had left in his old hide, and he waited patiently, watching the outlaws drink more and more. He kept his patience even while viewing the periodic ravishment of his great-granddaughter.

He settled his mind about the latter. There was nothing he could do about it at the moment. To try anything would bring only his own death—which mattered little to him any more—as well as that of Grace Red Bird. So he would not worry about it. He must wait, biding his time, until he could save Red Bird.

It was several hours, but the white men began to fall asleep one by one, collapsing with besotted groans where they sat. And even then Long Ridge waited, until he was sure all the men were sound asleep.

He stood up, wincing as his old bones squealed in protest at having been idle for so long. Long Ridge was torn between anger at the ravages of aging and humor at the odd ways his body protested even the smallest movements these days. He took a few minutes to stretch his arms and legs, trying to force his sluggish blood to move a little faster in his veins.

He lurched into the camp, not worried that he would be heard. The outlaws were far too drunk to hear him—unless he made too much noise. He fingered his Texas Dance revolver, wondering if he should just kill all the outlaws now and be done with it. But the feelings of inadequacy returned, and he was not sure he could kill them all before they got him. Then Red Bird would be in an even more difficult spot. He sighed, deciding to just spirit Red Bird out of camp and run for it.

He patted the butt of the Texas Dance one last time, remembering where it had come from. When the Confederates had come to Long Ridge's Cherokee village, they had laughed when the old man volunteered to fight. That had cut him to the quick, since in the offer to raise troops he had seen a chance to get back at the hated blue coats who had brought him to this foreign land. But the gray coats had laughed, and Long Ridge had slunk away, hurting inside with a humiliation so deep he never could have dreamed of it.

But he was proud when his grandson, Luther Spotted Bear, offered his services. Here was one, Long Ridge thought, who harkened back to the old days; a true warrior of the Cherokee people.

Spotted Bear left the village on Sallisaw Creek, bound and determined to revenge himself for the deaths of his father and mother on the Trail of Tears and for the humiliations the old ones like his grandfather had suffered. And he intended to see that his child, Grace Red Bird, would have a better life.

He came back less than a year later—in a pine box, to await burial. The Confederate captain who came to the village to talk about the death of Spotted Bear and several other of the village's young men gave Long Ridge the carbine and revolver Spotted Bear had carried.

Long Ridge sighed now in the darkness. He hefted the rifle in his left hand and stepped quietly toward Red Bird. The young woman was sleeping, though it was not the sleep of innocence and rest. Rather it was the sleep of someone haunted. She tossed and whimpered; she might be able to control herself in the face of these assaults on her body and soul while she was awake, but in the throes of unconsciousness, she had little protection.

Her dress had worked itself upward, uncovering her legs almost to the buttocks. Long Ridge shook his head as his stomach lurched from the sickness he felt at having known what she had gone through. He again briefly considered killing the outlaws before once more discarding the thought.

He knelt next to Red Bird. He clamped a hand over her mouth and shook her with the other. She awoke with a start, fighting even before her eyes were open. Long Ridge had a lot more in

BAD BLOOD

hand than he could safely handle, and he only hoped that she would quickly come to her senses and see who he was.

When she did, she stopped fighting. But by that time, he was exhausted and breathing heavily.

"What're you doin' here?" Red Bird asked in a hissing whisper, speaking English.

He rocked back on his heels and tried to speak, but he was having difficulty with it. Finally he managed to suck in enough air so that he could form words. "Came for you," he whispered, puffing.

Red Bird was almost shocked. She was, she knew, Long Ridge's favorite of his few remaining great-grandchildren. And he was a favorite of hers. She enjoyed listening to him talk of the old days and hearing his wisdom. But still, for him to have tracked these men down just to rescue her was almost beyond belief.

"We must go," he said quietly, his breathing almost back to normal.

Red Bird nodded and stood up. She offered her hand to her great-grandfather and helped pull him to his feet. "You have a horse?" Red Bird asked.

"Old Bess," Long Ridge answered, suddenly embarrassed.

"That old nag?" Red Bird asked in English, her own language insufficient to express her surprise and wonder in such a case.

Long Ridge only nodded, once again feeling the shame well up inside him.

Red Bird shrugged. The horse had gotten the old man here, and that was all that counted at the moment. "Where is she?"

Long Ridge pointed northeast, at a clump of brush. Red Bird nodded and headed off silently in that direction, Long Ridge following along. They got to the horse, and Long Ridge said, "We'd better steal you a horse and scatter the rest so they can't follow us."

"Good idea."

Leading Old Bess, they worked their way around the camp toward the outlaws' horses. "I'd like to kill them all, Grandfather," Red Bird said with a quiet hate that was almost startling in its intensity.

"I don't think we could get them all before they got us," Long Ridge said, almost sadly. *If only I was thirty years younger!* he thought. But he wasn't. They arrived at the small herd. Painfully and awkwardly, he climbed onto Bess's back. He drew his Texas Dance revolver, ready to set the horses to flight.

Red Bird rapidly began fashioning a rudimentary rein from a piece of rope to tie it to the lower jaw of one of the horses. But before she had finished, they heard a voice: "Goin' somewhere?"

Long Ridge cranked his head around so fast that it sent a spasm of pain shooting through him. One of the outlaws was standing there, grinning foolishly. He had his pistol out but he was holding it loosely, overconfident.

"Home," Red Bird said angrily, drawing the man's attention.

Long Ridge, whose revolver was hidden from the outlaw by his body, whipped the pistol up and fired three times.

The outlaw staggered under the impact of at least two pistol balls and fell. His finger jerked on the trigger reflexively, and the gun went off, but the bullet hit nothing but dirt.

Added to Long Ridge's shots, however, it did set the loose horses running. "Come on, Red Bird," Long Ridge roared, kicking Old Bess in the sides. Red Bird grabbed Long Ridge's hand and felt herself pulled up onto Old Bess as the workhorse rumbled out of the camp.

The two raced away as the other outlaws scrambled up from their blankets. Some shots were fired at the two fleeing Cherokees but with little effect, since the men were still either too drunk or too hungover to be able to aim.

Long Ridge and Red Bird rode hard, heading south to throw off any possible pursuit the white men might be able to mount. Eventually, they would turn east and then loop upward toward the north again, the direction in which they wanted to go. They did not spare the horse as they rode, though they had to slow considerably after a short while, because the old workhorse was not bred for speed or endurance running.

Along about dawn, when the light was deceptive, the great horse, puffing hard from the forced running, stepped into a chuckhole and fell forward almost onto her face. The two riders were flung headlong, and the horse squealed as her right foreleg snapped loudly.

"Damn!" exclaimed Long Ridge as he bounced to a halt on the dirt and dust. There were some ways of the white man, curses being one of them, that were much more suitable than Cherokee ways, he thought briefly. Long Ridge got up, thankful that none of his own old, fragile bones were broken. He looked about for Red Bird.

The young woman was sitting up, anger and humorous rue

flickering across her face. She stood up, too, asking, "You all right, Grandfather?"

He nodded, growing angry. Bess would have to be killed now, and that bothered him for two reasons. For one, he liked the faithful old workhorse; and second, they would be afoot now, in hostile territory, still miles and miles from their home. He doubted he could walk that far. He only hoped they could find an isolated ranch or farm and steal a couple of horses for the rest of the journey.

Taking a chance, Long Ridge reluctantly fired a ball into the horse's brain. By the time the echo had faded away, he had grabbed up his burlap sack of food supplies and taken the rifle from its scabbard. He took a few minutes to reload his pistol. With a shrug of resignation, he stepped off on foot, back straight, head held proudly.

Red Bird walked behind, comforted by her great-grandfather's presence but still watching him warily for any signs of strain.

They walked day after day. With each passing sun, Long Ridge grew a little weaker and could walk the next day with less determination and for less time. But also with each passing of the sun, they felt themselves a little safer—at least from the outlaws. There was no sign of pursuit; and, Long Ridge thought thankfully, little sign that Comanches or Kiowas were around.

He managed to kill a young buffalo one day, and they ate well of the fresh meat, though he was forced to expend some shot on keeping several wolves and coyotes at bay. They hurriedly jerked some of the meat over a slow, smoky fire for a day, so they would have rations that would last.

Once they did find a ranch and tried to sneak down and steal two horses. But a large, howling dog drove them away from the animals before Long Ridge could shoot the canine. By then, though, the house was aroused, and Long Ridge and Red Bird slunk off into the shadows that were quickly dispersing under the assault of the rising sun.

A week later, late in the day, Long Ridge stopped. He sniffed at the air, his head cocked.

"What is it?" Red Bird asked, sounding almost bored. She was tired and sore, still suffering from the degradations she had been dealt by the gang of outlaws.

"There's white men out there," Long Ridge said. "I can smell their fire."

"How can you tell it's white men?" Red Bird was beginning to think the old man had lost his mind.

"There's a difference between the way an Indian—any Indian—makes a fire and the way a white man makes a fire. And there's a difference in what white men cook."

"I don't smell anything," Red Bird said sullenly.

"Doesn't mean it's not there." Long Ridge had been angry, too, but suddenly he felt a spark of optimism.

Red Bird said nothing, but she also felt the tiniest flicker of hope growing inside her as she followed Long Ridge into the spreading darkness.

They moved silently, edging up through the brush toward the faint glow thrown by a fading fire. They had waited several hundred yards away while the talking of two men had died down. It was after midnight before they even began heading toward the three horses. They crept up slowly. The two men in this camp were not drunk, and, just from overhearing snatches of their conversation, Long Ridge knew the two whites were no strangers to traveling through dangerous land. They would, Long Ridge knew, be alert even in sleep. He wanted to make sure they were in the deepest of slumbers before trying anything.

Long Ridge nodded off, unable at his age to keep awake as long as he used to. When Red Bird finally woke him, Long Ridge realized it was not long before the daybreak. He stood up and rubbed his face, trying to erase the dullness of his sleep. He nodded, and they slipped forward, making no sound.

Long Ridge's respect for these two white men rose when he saw the quality of the three horses they had. He found a bit and bridle and eased up to a dark, powerful-looking black mustang. He slid the bit into the skittish horse's mouth. Just as he was about to pull himself wearily up onto the animal, a body flew out of the night and smashed into him.

Long Ridge went down, trying to fight but finding that all his breath and most of his strength had been slammed out of him. He fought as best as he could, hoping that Red Bird would be able to get away. Suddenly he found the muzzle of a pistol stuck under his nose and a young, hard voice telling him to ease off. He did.

With the telling of it, Long Ridge felt the slow burning of shame once again. He thought he was mostly over such things. He had been oppressed and feeling useless for so long that he did not think the shame still afflicted him. But it rose in him now as he sat, hands tied behind him, across the fire from this tall, fair-haired young man.

"You know, Mr. Long Ridge, not all whites are like Harlan Cross and his men. Some of us ain't, anyway."

"What'd you want us to do?" Long Ridge asked, half in anger, half in resignation. "Just walk up and ask for your horses?" He snorted derisively.

"Reckon that would've been foolish, wouldn't it?" Buck said reflectively. He sighed, wondering what to do with these two Cherokees. If he and Matt let them go, they might not live long enough to make it to their home. And they would be hanged for certain if they were turned over to the sheriff in the first town they found. "You hungry?" he asked, realizing that Long Ridge's tale had taken some hours and that it was near noon already.

CHAPTER
⋆ 5 ⋆

Matt Ramsey did not look happy, but, then, he hadn't looked—or been—happy for a while now. He looked at his younger brother and wondered about him. It seemed several lifetimes ago that Buck was a ten-year-old. Matt and his brother Kyle had just come home from the war, after a spell of imprisonment in Vicksburg. They encountered even more trouble back in New Liberty, in Fannin County, where Court Shelton and his son Gus had taken it upon themselves to run things in the area. But despite that trouble, Matt had usually managed to find time for Bucky, his favorite of his younger brothers.

Now Buck—no longer Bucky—sat across from him. Buck was seventeen, nearly as tall as Matt, though not as big across the shoulders and back. Matt Ramsey was a big man, the largest of the Ramseys. But he thought that in a few years, Buck would begin to rival him in size. Still, Buck had some of the youth left in him: his clear, innocent face; a mop of sandy, wild hair; gangly limbs.

Matt could want for no one—except possibly Kyle—better to be at his side in a fight, and it hurt him to know he was treating Buck the way he had been. But he was incapable of helping himself. He felt less than a man, what with the weakness brought on by his wound. His body was nearly healed, but the wounding of his soul—the coming so close to death and the having to have others do for him—cut him to the quick, filling him with doubts about himself and his manliness.

He scowled at Buck and said, "I'd just as soon we shoot 'em and be done with it."

Buck glared at Matt. He was once in awe of his big brother, but of late he had revised that opinion downward more than a little. He had always looked up to Matt, had always wanted to be like his big, broad-shouldered, dark-haired brother. But now he was almost contemptuous of Matt and the way Matt had been acting.

Mixed with that growing derision was a deep-seated fear. This behavior just wasn't the Matt he knew. He wondered—and worried—if Matt had perhaps given up on himself because of the wound, and that filled Buck with fear, for he did not know what to do to counter it. Matt had always been there for him—for all of them. But now . . .

"We can't do that, Matt, and you know it," Buck said evenly.

"Bah."

"Head on home then, if you're of a mind to, Matt," Buck said wearily. He was tired of all the tension of late. "I won't mind. But I aim to see these folks back to their homes."

"And you told 'em that, didn't you?" said Matt, only half trying to keep the sneer from his face.

"I did. But I told 'em I'd have to ask you. It comes to mind now that it ain't necessary to get your permission; just see if you want to come along."

"Reckon I'm of no mind to abet a couple of goddamn horse thieves," Matt said diffidently.

Buck had had enough of this nonsense from his brother. "What in the hell's eatin' at you, Matt?" he asked in accusatory tones. "You been grumpin' around all sour-faced since we left Justice. You don't want to do nothin'. You got no more compassion for folks that've come on hard times."

"Them Cherokees've brought their hard times on themselves. They're horse thieves, pure and simple."

"You should've sat and listened to their story, Matt," Buck said, trying to calm down. "I didn't explain it to you half so well as they did. They had more hard times of late than we've faced in our lives. They—"

"Don't you go tryin' to tell me about hard times, damnit," Matt growled.

Buck knew he was taking a chance, but he had to. "Oh," he said with a thick sneer, "poor ole Matt Ramsey took himself a Comanche arrow, and now all the world's got to listen to him whine and moan over it. Poor child almost died. Well, I reckon I'll just rig up a travois and throw your lazy butt on it so . . ."

The flames of hell leaped into Matt's eyes, almost burning Buck with their heat, and the younger Ramsey shut his mouth in a hurry. Matt stood, his fists clenched. It took all the inner resources he possessed to keep his hands at his sides, away from his pistol.

He turned to walk away, but Buck jumped up and grabbed Matt's left arm with his right hand, knowing he might be risking his life. "Stand and face it, Matt," Buck hissed. "Face whatever the hell's gnawin' at you. Stand and—"

Matt spun, launching a large fist at Buck's face as he did so. Buck managed to block it with his left forearm, but the power of it knocked him back a step. Fear seeped into his belly. Matt was bigger, stronger, and far more experienced in the deadly arts than Buck, and the younger Ramsey worried that he was in over his head. Matt could do some real damage to him if he put his mind to it. "Don't do that again, Matt," he warned, hoping his nervousness was not evident. "You're my big brother and all, but I ain't gonna stand here and get my butt kicked by you nor nobody."

Matt's rage towered so high he thought he'd explode with the intensity of it. Its force almost incapacitated him. He fought to bring it under control. Such rage—and the ineffectiveness it brought—could be deadly. He was afraid, though he would never admit that to anyone. Afraid that he could no longer control himself; afraid that he was not the man he was a few months ago; afraid that he would be a burden on everyone. He was torn inside, by the fear and by a spark of his old spirit, a simmering flame that would not let him give in all the way, either to his rage or to his despair.

Suddenly he spun on his heel and stomped off, leaving Buck standing there, amazed, startled, and worried. He took a step in the direction Matt had gone but stopped. Best leave Matt be for now, he thought. Sadly, and with a growing fear in him at what was becoming of his brother, he returned to the fire.

The pot of coffee from the noon meal was still hot, and Buck poured himself some, trying to ignore the eyes of the Cherokees on him. No one said anything as Buck sipped his coffee and the afternoon droned on. Buck half expected to hear Matt riding off, leaving them all here. He almost wished for that. Though Buck looked like his brother Kyle, he was more like Matt in temperament and action.

Matt Ramsey was a man who often gave of himself, trying to help family, friends, and people he did not even know. It seemed to be the way with all the Ramseys, though in Matt it was almost a calling. Buck was much the same, and after hearing the story of the two Cherokees, he wanted to help John Long Ridge and the attractive Grace Red Bird. It was why he had gone to talk to Matt earlier. Now he almost hoped Matt *would* ride off, leaving them. That way Buck could help the Cherokees without concern for what Matt thought.

"You're a goddamn fool, Buck," Matt said from behind him, breaking his young brother's reverie.

Buck swiveled his head to look at Matt.

"Such people ain't worth our efforts." He was calm, though still depressed. And he was filled with self-disgust at his earlier treatment of Buck.

"That's the first time I ever heard you talk against Indians, Matt," Buck said warily.

"I don't give a hoot that they're Indians, Buck," Matt said quietly. "But I don't cotton to horse thieves, no matter their color."

"They're just folks fallen on hard times, Matt," Buck said, hope springing up within him.

"I reckon. But I still think you're a goddamn fool for wantin' to help 'em."

"The Good Lord won't hold with such thinkin', Matt," Buck said, almost embarrassed. He had let his churchgoing fall off a spell since his parents had died some years before, and this occasionally filled him with guilt.

Matt shrugged. "That don't change my thinkin'." He paused, squatting next to his brother and staring at the two Cherokees. "But I reckon you're bound and set on doin' this." It was almost a question.

"I am," Buck said firmly.

Matt was trying to make amends, and he was not used to doing such a thing. He was too prideful a man to apologize easily. "Then I reckon I'll help you." There was no contrition in his voice.

Buck looked happy, but his face froze when Matt said, "But I'll tell you this, Buck: At the first sign of trouble, I aim to shoot both these horse-stealin' varmints down." He was speaking to Buck, but he still looked straight at the two Indians.

"They'll not give us any trouble," Buck said, with more confidence that he really felt. He looked away from his brother to Red Bird and then Long Ridge. "Will you, folks?" He smiled warmly.

"No," Long Ridge said solemnly.

"No," Red Bird offered, though bitterness dripped from her voice.

"I'll get the horses ready," Buck said, tossing the remains of his coffee into the fire. He set the cup down and started to rise.

"No need," Matt said, stopping Buck halfway up. Buck looked at him, an itch of worry starting. "It's too late in the day, Buck," his brother explained softly.

He did not know why he had changed his mind about helping Long Ridge and Red Bird. He had stalked off after his run-in with Buck and went to sit down by the creek. The burbling of the water and the soft hum of insects comforted him and eased his inner pain some. He had begun to feel like a fool for acting the way he had and for almost fighting his brother. He had resolved to try to be more like his old self. And he had always harbored a soft spot inside for people to whom life had dealt a poor hand.

"These folks've traveled long and hard on foot, and they need some rest." Matt did not mention that he was in no mood for more traveling right now; that his chest hurt and the pain wore him down. "Mornin'll be soon enough."

Buck brightened considerably, thinking Matt might be over whatever had been plaguing him.

Matt managed a wan grin. "And I reckon it's nigh onto suppin' time."

"You're hungry?" Buck asked, surprised. It was the first time since Matt was wounded that he had shown a real interest in food.

"Yep." Matt was lying. He had no real desire to eat, though he knew he needed food. Still, it would make Buck feel better that he seemed to want a meal.

"Comin' right up." Buck had squatted back down, but now he stood up all the way, looking pleased. Maybe life would get back to normal, now that Matt was acting himself again. Buck hurried off to get food. After he had prepared it and set it to cooking, he looked at Long Ridge and Red Bird.

"Think you could untie us, now that you and your brother are fixin' to help us?" Long Ridge asked.

"Matt, what do you think?"

"Reckon they'll not be goin' anywhere," Matt allowed. He did not fully trust the Indians, but now that he had decided on a course of action, he was willing to allow some leeway. "But," he added, looking at Long Ridge, "I don't expect you'll be needin' your gun or knife back for a spell, neither."

Long Ridge nodded seriously. Buck walked around the fire and untied Long Ridge, then Red Bird. Then he whispered, "I'm puttin' a heap of faith in you two." He was suddenly not so sure that what he was doing was right. "Matt don't trust you none, and with some good reason. He means what he says when he told you he'd shoot you down at the first sign of trouble." Buck stepped back.

"Mind if we stand?" Long Ridge asked. "We been settin' a long time, and these old bones could use some movement before they get set in stone." He tried to chuckle but couldn't quite make it.

"Stand and move all you want," Buck said, mostly amiably. "Just keep away from the horses—and our supplies. Both of you."

Long Ridge nodded. He started to rise but was having trouble. With a look of sadness, Buck helped, lifting Long Ridge under the arms. He hoped he would never get this old and helpless.

"Thank you, boy," Long Ridge said, bitterness wrenching his guts. He would never get used to the infirmities that came with age, especially since there seemed to be new ones coming each day. He sighed.

Red Bird had stood and was walking toward the bushes to tend to personal needs. She stopped and looked at her great-grandfather and the young white man helping him. She felt a touch of affection. Buck Ramsey was helping out of some innate goodness, not from any sense of superiority, she noticed. It pleased her, and *that* worried her.

"Need more help, Mr. Long Ridge?" Buck asked calmly.

"No, thanks, boy," Long Ridge said with as much dignity as he could muster under the circumstances.

Buck nodded and went back to the fire. Red Bird was already off in the brush; Matt had slipped off, too, down toward the creek to be by himself. Buck squatted and checked on the bubbling pot of beans and the frying pan of sizzling bacon. He was getting plumb tired of the same meal every day, but it was about all they had left, and even that was running a mite low. He would have to keep an eye out for antelope or deer or even rabbit when they rode on.

He sat back onto his behind, wrapping his arms around his knees. He looked with a slight smile at Long Ridge, who was walking stiff-legged back and forth, trying to work the kinks out of old muscles and joints.

"Supper's on," he called after a while.

CHAPTER
★ 6 ★

James Buchanan Ramsey gulped in fear. Matt was going to kill him sure as the sun rose when he found out. For a moment, Buck considered running. Just taking off and high-tailing it for parts unknown as fast as his long legs could take him. But he cast that thought aside. He was a Ramsey, by God, and Ramseys did not run from something that was uncomfortable and unpleasant, especially if it was trouble of his own making. He sighed and went to wake Matt, ready to face his brother's wrath.

It took Matt a few minutes to come awake, once again making Buck wonder what was wrong with the older Ramsey; and once again angering Matt himself.

"It mornin' already?" Matt asked, sitting up. Tiredness seemed to sit on him like a set of longjohns.

"Nearabout," Buck said noncommittally. Just because he knew he had to tell his brother, and just because he was ready to face the consequences, did not mean he was eager to do either.

"Breakfast ready?" Matt thought it a good sign that he was asking about food.

"Coffee's on, but I ain't got to breakfast yet."

"Why?" Matt reached for his boots and began pulling them on. Now that he had made his decision to help the two Cherokees, he was feeling a little better about himself. Not much, but a little.

"Somethin' I got to tell you," Buck muttered, embarrassed. He felt a slice of iciness in his bowels.

"What's that?" Matt stood up, rolling his shoulders to get the blood moving against the morning chill. It was still dark, though gray streaks of light broke the gloom somewhat. Once again the camp was covered with a soft wrapper of mist rising from the creek.

Buck gulped again, forcing back the fear. He was not so much afraid that Matt would beat him up; what did frighten him was the look in Matt's eyes he expected to receive. The look of disappointment, the look that said "I put my trust in you, Buck, and you let me down." He did not want to see that look and would have done anything in his power to avoid seeing it. But it would have to be.

"The Cherokees are gone, Matt," he said in a rush.

Matt stopped rolling his shoulders and stared at Buck, who winced. The look in Matt's eyes was as bad as he had expected. He felt lower than a snake's bellybutton.

"Gone?" Matt repeated, his voice cracking with surprise and anger.

"Gone."

"They take anything?" Matt was holding himself on a very tight rein only with a great deal of difficulty.

"The horses," Buck squawked in self-disgust. He waited for the explosion.

"Jesus, Buck!" Matt said scornfully. "How could you have been so damned stupid. I told you that wantin' to help them horse-thievin' bastards was foolish. Lord, Buck, it's . . . you're . . ." He was beside himself with anger and contempt and so sputtered to a halt.

Buck stood silently, scuffling the toe of one boot in the dirt and feeling like he was a schoolboy again and in trouble for one of the pranks he and his three year-older brother, Luke, were so fond of playing. He wanted to say something, to try to explain that what he had done was right, but he knew the words would only make the situation worse and anger Matt all the more.

Matt paced off a few steps, giving his anger some moments to percolate to the right texture of doneness. But in the doing, he found to his surprise that it also gave him time to develop an anger at himself. An anger at having gone along with this; and an anger at not having been strong enough to have stopped this.

"I can't believe," Matt went on, ignoring the self-disgust and choosing to focus his anger on Buck for the time being, "that you were so damned stupid. Or that you didn't hear 'em. Jesus, Buck, now we're out here in the middle of nowhere, miles from our place down on the Trinity, with no horses. I don't know about you, dammit, but I ain't fond of walkin' miles on end because my brother was so goddamn, flap-ass stupid as to let two Indians—a goddamn old man who can't barely stand up and an itchy-foot girl—just ride off with our horses, pretty as you please without so much as a thank you, boys, for the critters. I just can't . . ."

Buck tried to blot out the torrent of words, to keep his head above the flood tide of sentiment. But he couldn't. Seeing that look of disgust in Matt's eyes had been every bit as horrible as he had imagined. And if Matt had stopped at that, Buck would have swallowed his tongue before saying anything. But no, Matt had to go on a rampage of words, and Buck was not about to sit and meekly accept that. Especially when Matt was, when one thought about it, as much to blame as Buck himself was.

"Now hold on a minute here, Matt," Buck said finally, the words popping out with force and determination.

Matt's river of babble stopped as if dammed, and he stood, mouth agape, looking at his brother. "What's that you said, boy?" Matt demanded.

"You heard me. You been speechifyin' like you were runnin' for office here. Words comin' out like you was gonna die the second you shut up. And not sayin' a damn thing."

"Like hell." Matt glared at Buck. "I ought to just whomp the tar out of you, boy, for puttin' us in such a fix."

"As if you didn't have nothin' to do with it," Buck said defiantly.

"It was you decided to act like some guardian angel and help them woeful folks out."

"And it was you who agreed to help."

The two men glared at each other, each knowing he was partly to blame; neither wanting to admit it; both reluctant to lay the full blame on the other. Buck was a little concerned about Matt, knowing his brother had not been himself of late. That worried the younger Ramsey, who thought it possible Matt just might attack him. Matt had come close to doing so once already.

Matt considered that possibility but discarded it. The feelings of doubt, which he thought he might be getting over at last, had rushed back into him, like a flash flood in a desert wash. He felt inadequate, useless. He should have heard the Cherokees stealing their horses—both this time and the day before. But he hadn't, and now he wanted badly to take his feelings of inadequacy out on his younger brother.

Well, he decided, he ought not to take such things out on Buck, at least until he had calmed down some and could think a little more clearly about his brother. The ones he should take it out on were the horse thieves. And he decided at that moment that he would catch them. "Get breakfast goin', boy," he growled.

"Ain't much left."

"Then make what there is."

"Yessir." Buck hurried off to do what he was told. Matt came up to the fire, sticking out his hands to warm them a little after a few minutes. "What're you plannin' to do, Matt?" Buck asked cautiously.

Matt was still rankled, but he forced himself to keep at least outwardly calm. "I'm goin' after them redskin bastards."

"It's gonna be a long walk."

"Don't matter. They got that black mustang of mine. You know how I feel about that horse, Buck. I caught that horse, broke it to saddle, and then couldn't bring myself to sell it 'cause it was such a good animal. I ain't about to let them savages get away with that horse—or kill it tryin' to get back to their home."

"Want company?"

"If you think you can refrain from doin' any more good deeds for a spell."

"I can't promise, Matt," Buck said, grinning a little, experimenting. "Hell, such things're in my blood. Yours, too," he added, his grin widening minutely.

"Bah!"

Buck knew he had scored a point with his brother, who was not willing to admit to his basic decency and desire to help those less fortunate than himself.

They hurriedly ate the last of the bacon with some beans. Then they began packing. "We got only enough beans for about one more meal, Matt," Buck said apologetically.

But Matt was wrapped up in thoughts of the chase already, and he only grunted an acknowledgment.

In less than an hour after Buck had awoken Matt, the two men strode off on foot, following the trail of their horses northeastward. Each had his saddle and saddle blanket, with scabbard, saddlebags, and bedroll attached, slung over his left shoulder, leaving their right hands free for their pistols, should they need them.

Matt marched along at a good clip, feeling pretty good physically. But his mind was still troubled by the disturbing thoughts he had had since being wounded. And it was capped by the anger at the situation in which he found himself. The long, lonely miles of walking gave Matt ample time for building up his anger and his self-loathing. He fluctuated from one emotion to the other and then back.

Matt had some money on him, and he hoped as he walked that he and Buck would find a town soon. If they did that, he would have enough for a couple of horses, and they could be on the trail quickly, the way they should be. And with each ridge or hill they climbed, he would stop and scan the desolate countryside, looking for any telltale signs of a town or even a ranch.

But he was greeted with nothing at each one. He never even saw a road that might lead somewhere. By the time they made camp that night, not having eaten a noonday meal, Matt was almost gray with fatigue. He would not let on, but his chest hurt considerably, and he was weak and shaking. He said a silent prayer of thanks when they found a copse of scrub oak that would make a decent campsite for the night.

They ate fairly well, saving their beans for an emergency and dining, instead, on the two jackrabbits that Buck had brought down with his Winchester during the afternoon. Right after eating, Matt crawled into his blankets, not caring what Buck thought about such an action, and fell asleep.

Buck stared at the inert form for a little while, wondering again what demons his brother was battling. Then he, too, turned in. It had been a long, hard day, and there seemed to be no relief in sight.

The next day offered more of the same. Step after dusty step, Matt began slowing down somewhere in the late morning, until he was doing little more than shuffling. Buck wanted to help, but he knew that Matt would not accept the help even if he offered. So he kept his mouth shut and slowed his pace to match that of his brother.

They camped in the open that night, making a pitiful fire of buffalo chips, over which they cooked the last of their beans and the last of their coffee. They saved enough of the latter to have at least a mugful each in the morning. Buck regretted missing the only shot he had taken that afternoon at another jackrabbit. But the speedy hare was more than a hundred yards off and running flat out, zigzagging. The only good thing about their camp was the tiny trickle of water that might have been a creek at some point. It allowed them to fill their canteens, though it took a lot of time, and have some water for their coffee.

Then it was back to walking, feeling the searing heat of the sun trying to smite them down. It was a brutal, taxing heat that enveloped and smothered them, threatening to squeeze the life out of them.

Buck glanced frequently at Matt, worrying more and more about the older Ramsey. Matt looked about done in. "What're you fixin' to do when we catch them Cherokees, Matt?" Buck finally asked about midmorning. He hoped that if he could fire Matt up about something, it might make his brother's going a little easier.

"Kill 'em," Matt murmured, the words thick from his dry mouth.

"You sure you don't want to help 'em?"

"Help 'em?" Matt echoed, his eyes sparking. "Why in hell should I do such a thing?" he demanded. "Lord, Buck, you're a fool sometimes. Was I gonna do that, I'd do just as well to shoot myself here and now and save everybody a heap of trouble. No"—he shook his head with angry jerks—"I aim to see that Mr. John Long Ridge don't ever steal another horse."

"And Miss Red Bird?" The thought of her, beyond the fact that she had stolen his horse, was a pleasant one for Buck. Even more pleasant than thinking about Miss Eula Mae McFarrin. After all, thinking about Eula Mae was painful, since she had cast him over.

"A horse thief's a horse thief, no matter whether it's a he or a she."

But to Buck he did not sound so certain. And Buck still wanted to try to help the Cherokees. He wasn't sure why, but he thought it had something to do with the fact that the two of them had suffered so much at the hands of whites that Buck wanted to show them that some palefaces could be good people.

They walked on silently, Matt seemingly having gained a little strength in the short exchange.

Just after noon, Buck stopped. Matt, following a few paces behind, almost ran into his brother, since he was not paying much attention. He looked at Buck, who stood with his head cocked, as if listening for something. Matt let his saddle fall. He rubbed his shoulder as he, too, listened. Suddenly his eyes narrowed. "I hear it," he whispered.

"What is it?" Buck asked.

"A stage. Close by. Come on." He grabbed his saddle and ran off.

CHAPTER
7

Matt and Buck clambered their way up a hill of crumbling, grass-covered dirt, scrabbling for hand- and footholds in the rolling soil. As they neared the top, they dropped their saddles. They flattened and crawled the last several yards, pulling themselves up to the crest cautiously. Matt was breathing heavily and looked rather pale. Buck had a momentary flash of fear that his brother's puffing would be loud enough to be heard by those down below.

Buck lay in the sweltering heat, staring down. A Butterfield stage—Buck guessed it was on the Fort Sill to Jacksboro run—was stopped. The driver and shotgun rider sat on the high seat, arms in the air. The passengers—a drummer of some kind, a gambler, by the looks of him, two cowpokes, and an enormous, unattractive older woman—stood just outside the open door of the stagecoach.

Three men, wearing long canvas dusters and bandanna masks, trained guns on the people. One sat on a horse, holding a double-barreled shotgun on the driver and rider. He was partly hidden from the Ramseys' view by a cottonwood tree. The two other outlaws were on foot and held pistols. One stood back a little, watching over the passengers, while the other took whatever valuables he could find from them. A strongbox lay on the ground, where the driver had tossed it. Two saddled horses were tied to a bush back behind the outlaws a short way.

Buck shoved his hat back a little and wiped the sweat from his forehead. As he ran his hand over a pants leg, he surveyed the lay of the land. It was, he decided, a fine place for a stage holdup. The stage would have to drive between this hill and one directly across. The two ridges seemed to run on for half a mile or more. The opposite one was pocked with holes, while trees and boulders lay thick along the base, providing good hiding places. Buck assumed the ridge he and Matt were on looked the same, though he was not about to hang over the edge to stare down the seemingly sheer cliff of it. The Ramseys were about sixty feet up on the ridge top and maybe a hundred yards from the stage.

"Well, Matt?" Buck asked. "Reckon we ought to do somethin' about all this?"

"Those folks ain't nothin' to us."

"Yeah, but . . ."

Suddenly Matt grinned grimly. "But those boys do have horses we could use. You take the one takin' the stuff from the people; I'll get the other on foot. We'll worry about that third one later. Maybe our fire'll drive him out where we can get a good shot at him."

"Just make sure you hit the one you're shootin' at," Buck joshed, not looking at his brother, so he did not see the scowl flicker on Matt's face and then disappear.

"You do the same," Matt growled. "You shoot one of them passengers by mistake, and your—and my—butt's gonna be in a heap of trouble."

"You ever seen me miss at this range?" Buck asked defensively, his voice rising a notch in intensity.

James Buchanan Ramsey was the best rifle shot Matt had ever seen. The Winchester seemed to be an extension of the young man, much the way the Colt was with Matt.

"Not 'cept for that jackrabbit yesterday," Matt ribbed.

"Shoot," Buck drawled quietly in annoyance. He slid the Winchester up. He levered a round into the chamber and rested his cheek comfortably on the stock. He followed the one man with his sights. "You set, Matthew?" he asked.

"Yep."

Buck took a breath and held it as he started to squeeze the trigger. At the same time, he mentally braced himself for the report of Matt's rifle next to him, not wanting to flinch at the wrong time. He fired and, an instant later, heard Matt's Winchester.

The outlaw who was collecting valuables from the passengers was knocked forward into the front wheel of the stage, where he bounced off and fell down. A bright red stain was already spreading across his back as the report of the shot echoed back from the ridge opposite the Ramseys.

The other outlaw on foot jerked but did not fall. "Dammit!" Matt exploded. He had only winged the man. Matt snapped the lever of his Winchester down and back up to fire again.

The outlaw had slapped his left hand onto the sudden wound high up on his right arm. It was not bad enough to have knocked the gun out of his hand. He half turned, wondering where the shooting was coming from, and got knocked sideways off his feet by the impact of Matt's second bullet. He struggled to get up, but none of his muscles worked right, and he collapsed.

At the first sound of firing, the mounted outlaw fired his shotgun at the driver. But the surprise of the gunfire had caused him to twitch, and the dose of buckshot only shredded the wood at the top of the coach behind the seat.

The driver, on the side of the stage away from the outlaws, jumped over the side. The shotgun guard leaped at the mounted outlaw. He was clubbed aside by the masked man as the outlaw swung the shotgun with his right hand and jerked his reins with the other. He jabbed spurs into the horse's side and tore off just as Matt fired his second shot at the other outlaw.

As the mounted outlaw raced off, Buck shoved himself up into a kneeling position. "Stay down, Matt!" he snapped. He fired, levered, and fired again. He felt a moment's satisfaction when he saw the fleeing outlaw flinch. But the man did not stop and was soon around a curve in the trail, behind an outcropping of the ridge. "Damn," Buck muttered.

Matt, still prone, had nonetheless been able to watch. "Don't worry about it, Buck," he said gruffly. "You winged him. Maybe he won't make it too far."

"I should've had him, Matt," Buck groused. He would not accept that the man was riding hard and bobbing, bent over his horse, and that Buck's footing was not very steady on the dirt cliff. He felt he should have gotten the outlaw cleanly.

Buck stood up and held out a hand to Matt. The older Ramsey took it and let himself be helped up. This was not a time he would—or could—feel out of place in accepting help. It was a friendly gesture on his brother's part and not a sign of weakness on his own. Buck pointed, and Matt nodded. They grabbed their gear and headed for what looked to be a steep, eroded trail heading downward.

It was tricky going, but they were soon on the flat and walking swiftly toward the stage. Matt squared his big shoulders and made sure he was walking tall. He'd be damned if he'd let these people see any sign of weakness in him.

The woman was back inside the coach, her blubbery face pasty with fright. Everyone else was gathered around one or the other of the bodies. The guard had gotten up and was standing, hat in hand, holding a bandanna to a cut over his temple. The driver stood with him, talking softly but keeping a wary eye on his surroundings. He spotted Matt and Buck and reached for his gun. Then he realized they must have been the ones who had killed the two outlaws. He issued a warning, and everyone turned to face the two Ramseys.

The driver stepped out to greet them, his hand held out. "Lord, but I'm glad to meet you boys," he said, relief evident on his face. He was a hard man, but this was the third time he had been the victim of a holdup like this, and he was not at all happy with that. "I'm Hap Cosgrove."

"Matt Ramsey," the dark-haired brother said, shaking Cosgrove's hand. "My brother Buck." Those two also shook hands.

"What're you boys doin' out here afoot?" Cosgrove asked.

"Lost our mounts," Buck said before Matt could launch into a tirade, which Buck suspected he was about to do. "We been hoofin' it more'n two days."

"Be glad to give you boys a ride down to Jacksboro. It's the least we could do in the way of thanks."

"Hell, yes," the guard said. He stuffed the bloody bandanna into a hip pocket and came up to shake hands with both Ramseys. "Name's Tobe McWhirter." He paused, then said, "Weren't for you boys, no tellin' what would've happened to us all."

"Know who they were?" Matt asked. He was not really interested, but he felt a little embarrassed under the spotlight of gratitude.

"Got no clue."

"This one's Pace Hansen," the gambler offered, tapping one body's side with his boot.

The Ramseys dropped their saddles and followed McWhirter and Cosgrove to where the gambler stood. Someone had pulled down the masks of both dead outlaws. "You know him?" Matt asked.

"Seen him before. Played cards against him one night up in the Nations. Seen wanted posters on him, too. Mean bastard. But dumb. Usually rides with Harlan Cross and that bunch."

Matt and Buck looked at each other. "How about the other one?" Matt asked.

"Never saw him before. But I think the one that took off is Garrick O'Fallon. A real hardcase that one, if he's O'Fallon. Favors that scattergun he was carryin'. He also rides with Cross most often."

"Why do you think that's who it is?" Buck asked. "His face was covered."

"The hat. I've seen posters of O'Fallon, too. Always wears a gray derby, with a gold figure of an eagle pinned on the front. It was, I've heard, the way Cross and his band of guerrillas distinguished themselves to each other during the war."

Matt shrugged. It was of no concern to him. Buck stood quietly, thoughtfully.

"Well, how about it, gents?" Cosgrove asked. "You boys want a ride into Jacksboro? Or anywhere else along the line?" He fidgeted a bit. "I'm fallin' behind schedule and got to get back on the road here before long."

Matt rubbed his cheek and chin, both covered with several days' worth of stubble. "I'd just as soon take their horses, if you don't mind," he said softly. But his eyes were hard, as if daring Cosgrove or anyone else to challenge him.

But Cosgrove was not even looking at Matt when he said, "I got no problem with that, Mr. Ramsey." He turned from considering McWhirter's wound to face the brothers. "We owe you a heap, and I got no call for them horses. Don't expect none of these others do, either."

"You boys mind if we take the horses?" Matt said to the two cowboys.

Both shook their heads. They had already retrieved their pistols and were rolling cigarettes; they wanted only to get back on the trail. They had no valuables and only a few dollars between them. They had taken that back from the dead outlaw and passed around everyone else's valuables.

Matt nodded. "Then that's all the thanks we need, Mr. Cosgrove. Y'all have a safe journey the rest of the way."

Cosgrove grinned wanly. "I could do with that." He turned to McWhirter. "Think you can climb up top by yourself, Tobe?"

"Yep."

Cosgrove nodded. "You two cowpokes there, come help me get them bodies in the boot."

"What for?" one asked, not exactly thrilled at the prospect of work.

"I want to bring 'em to Jacksboro. There might be a reward on 'em. I reckon the Ramseys here deserve it, but . . ."

"Split it between y'all," Matt said. "Me and Buck don't need it."

Cosgrove nodded, and the two cowboys seemed to perk up considerably. While they went to work, Matt walked to where the two outlaws' horses were tied. He talked to them softly, wanting to gain the trust of the animals. Buck came along, doing the same. Matt naturally gravitated to a large, chesty bay gelding with a white blaze on his forehead. Buck looked over the other, a dark chestnut gelding with four white stockings.

Within a few minutes, the Ramseys had the horses feeling comfortable with them. They stripped off the old saddles and gear, tossing it all aside, before putting on their own saddles and blankets. That done, Matt began going through the outlaws' gear. He took out some paper cartridges for his Colt and whatever food he found—bacon, beans, coffee, sugar, a little cornmeal, and a bit of flour.

Buck began carrying the outlaws' gear to the stagecoach, where Cosgrove stowed it in the boot with the bodies. Finished, he and Matt mounted and trotted over to the coach. Cosgrove and the two cowboys were just tying down the canvas covering over the boot.

The driver looked up. He straightened, squinting up at the Ramseys. "You sure we can't do somethin' more for you boys?" He felt a little guilty about the reward.

"Nope," Matt said.

"But the reward and all . . ."

"Hell," Matt said with a low chuckle. "These boys ain't the Youngers. The reward's likely to be maybe twenty bucks apiece for 'em. These horses're worth more'n that. We've got what we need."

"If you're sure . . ." He figured the reward was at least fifty dollars each, which wasn't so bad, even divided up some.

"Yep," Buck said.

"Come on, Buck," Matt said impatiently. "It's time we was back on the trail. Time's a wastin'."

"Thanks again, boys," Cosgrove said. The two cowboys nodded briefly in gratitude.

Matt touched his hat brim and spurred his horse on. Buck did the same, and then the two Ramsey brothers were loping up the road.

CHAPTER
★ 8 ★

"I've got to stop, Granddaughter," John Long Ridge said. He was tired beyond belief; his rear end hurt from his time on horseback; his bones ached; and his stomach was twisted from hunger.

"We must push on, Grandfather," Grace Red Bird said, with a frightened glance behind her.

"I can't." Long Ridge stopped his horse and sat on it, puffing. The black mustang seemed unaffected by the fact that it had been going without stop for almost three days. He bent over, resting his hands on the horse's neck where it met the torso. "We have come far. And they are afoot. They cannot catch us."

Red Bird was uncertain. She had suffered so much at the hands of the outlaw gang that she was fearful of all men. Even the two they had stolen these horses from. The Ramseys were good men, she thought, but still . . . The older one—the big man with the broad shoulders, shock of black hair, and glittering, dark eyes—was the one she was afraid of. He had a deadly look about him. But beyond that, he also had the look of a man who no longer cared. He would kill her and her great-grandfather without compunction, she thought.

The younger, fair-haired one, Buck, was a nice boy, and under different circumstances she might not have been averse to having the youth come courting. But the lingering fear inspired by Harlan Cross and his men had made her wary of any and all whites, even a fresh-faced, seemingly innocent one like Buck Ramsey.

She finally decided, though, that Long Ridge was right. They had ridden hard at first, then slowed to conserve the horses' strength. But they had not stopped since they'd left the Ramseys' camp, except twice to eat hurried meals. Before he had tried to steal the black mustang the first time, Long Ridge had set his carbine down. Buck did not know about it and so did not look for the weapon. When he and Red Bird took off, Long Ridge made sure he had grabbed the rifle. It was the only weapon, other than a small knife, that they had, since Buck had taken Long Ridge's pistol and big knife right off. He had managed to bring down an antelope with the rifle the first afternoon, and he and Red Bird had lived off that since.

Red Bird pointed to a clump of stunted cedars. Long Ridge looked up, his eyes bleary from age and tiredness. He nodded and straightened. They trotted toward the copse. Long Ridge slid off his horse, his legs barely able to hold him up. He made water and then lay down, head cradled on his arms. He was asleep in moments.

Red Bird looked down at her great-grandfather with affection. She smiled softly as she began to curry the horses. The sun was making a blaze of color across the sky when she finished the horses and began gathering loose wood. She made up a fire and set a piece of antelope meat on a flat rock in the flames. The meat was going bad and would probably be unusable tomorrow. But it would do for now, Red Bird decided, and keep them alive. Perhaps tomorrow they could shoot another one or, even better, maybe a buffalo. Her mouth watered as she thought of the taste of fresh buffalo meat.

She sighed. Such hopes were foolish. If they got a buffalo, all well and good. If they did not, they would have to live on whatever they could. Wishing about it would not make it so.

As she waited for the meat to cook, Red Bird looked down at herself. Her calico dress was in tatters and was fouled with various sorts of grime. She smiled, thinking that she would like to just tear it off and burn it—and with it the memories of what those beasts had done to her—and just go about buck naked. But that would shock her poor old great-grandfather and give anyone they met the wrong ideas. She shuddered at that.

With the small knife, she flipped the piece of meat over and sat back again, glancing at Long Ridge. He was an amazing man to her. Seventy-six years old and the only one of her people to come for her. There were times on their journey after escaping from Cross that she felt a surge of anger at the old man. He couldn't keep up, he tired easily, he complained too much about aches and pains—half of them imagined, thought Red Bird in her angrier moments. But in thinking on it now, Long Ridge had accomplished far more than most men half his age would have. As far as she was concerned, Long Ridge had earned the right to complain about anything that caught his fancy. She resolved to be more patient with him, more caring. He deserved it.

The meat was done, she decided, and she pulled it away from the flames on the point of her knife. She waved it in the air to cool it before sinking her teeth into it. When she finished, she got their only canteen and drank carefully. There was not much water left, and she wanted to make sure Long Ridge would have some when he awoke.

Long Ridge was a little more chipper in the morning, having slept the night away. He grumbled at the poor quality of the meat, but he ate it nonetheless. After eating, he said, "We should stay here another day or two. I need more rest."

"We can't, Grandfather," Red Bird said softly. "We have little meat left, and that will be inedible soon. And we have only the water in our canteen. We must ride on and find a place where we can have water. And perhaps you can hunt along the way." She smiled warmly. "You are a great hunter, John Long Ridge, and you will find us buffalo."

Long Ridge grinned, pride surging through his thin chest. The thought of having fresh buffalo was good; but the thought of traveling was not. Still, it could not be helped.

They pushed onward, moving slowly, Red Bird wanting to make the trip as easy as possible for Long Ridge. The old warrior did not get a buffalo, but he did manage to bring down a black-tailed deer in the late morning. Just before noon, they found a spot along the Wichita River that would make a nice camp. There were tall, sturdy cottonwoods that would provide wood, as well as shade from the oppressive sun. The river was running well, so fresh water was plentiful. There was enough brush to keep them screened from passersby, should any come along, but not so much as to make the spot unlivable. Even the riverbank was strewn with sand and small pebbles, rather than mud.

Red Bird looked at Long Ridge. The old man nodded once. She smiled and returned it. They set about making their camp.

BAD BLOCK

• • •

For the most part, the two Ramseys rode quietly. They spoke only when necessary, though on several occasions Buck caught his brother muttering threats against the Cherokees they were following.

Several hours after they left the stagecoach—only minutes after they turned off the road and headed crosscountry—rain began to fall. The temperature dropped, and a light wind blew up. Buck was thankful they still had their slickers. The soft rain would have been comforting, Matt thought, if it weren't washing away the trail of the Cherokees. It would make finding the two Indians much harder, Matt figured.

As if reading his mind, Buck said, "We'll find 'em, Matt. Don't you fret."

"Hell, we ain't gonna be able to track 'em with this rain."

"We know which way they're goin'. We'll be able to track 'em."

But the scowl stayed on Matt's face.

They stumbled onto an old adobe house—abandoned for decades, they supposed, from the look of it—and decided to spend the night there. Though great parts of the old house were falling in, it would still offer them a relatively dry place. They made a torch from a ripped up shirt wound around a stick and entered the house. It took several minutes of steady gunfire to rid the place of snakes, rats, and other critters.

Buck brought the horses inside, unsaddled, and tended to them, while Matt set about gathering what fuel he could. He found an old broken chair, several small, dry logs, and more than a few buffalo and cow chips inside the structure and piled them in a dry corner to make a fire. He even decided to make their meal—more bacon and beans—which shocked Buck. But the younger Ramsey said nothing.

It was still raining in the morning when Buck awoke. He was up first, and he stood looking down at his brother for a bit. Matt looked peaceful in sleep, but there was a little bit of an unnatural pallor about him. It was, Buck decided, probably from too much exertion and too much riding of late. It would pass.

Buck hoped Matt would begin to mend soon. The worst, obviously, was past, but it was more than two months since Matt had been wounded. The physical effects could be expected to linger this long—and even longer. But Matt seemed to have given up on himself, and that bothered Buck to no end. It was that healing that he hoped would begin soon.

Buck set about making breakfast. The smell of the coffee woke Matt, who sat up and almost smiled at the wonderful smell. He would have been happy, except that he still felt pangs that told him he should have been the first one up.

Matt ate with more of an appetite than he had shown in a long time. "You're gonna make a hell of a wife for someone one of these days, Buck," he commented, trying to achieve some of his old humor.

Buck flamed with embarrassment, but he retorted, "Least I don't take half the night just to rassle down one scrawny little Indian girl."

Hurt and anger grabbed Matt by the throat, and for a moment he thought he could not breathe. He knew his brother was joshing him, and he could accept that. But the inadequacy he had been feeling for so long now turned it from a humorous riposte to something almost threatening. Matt struggled for control of his emotions, finally making some headway. "Well," he said, his voice touched with bitterness, "you didn't do so well neither, taking so much effort to bring down Long Ridge, who's ten years older'n the Good Lord himself."

"Shoot," Buck said with a grin, not hearing the hurt in Matt's voice. "I just didn't want to hurt him any."

"You're lucky you didn't soil your britches," Matt growled.

"Hmmph," Buck grumbled, but he was secretly pleased at the banter. It was almost like the old days. He was unaware of how much pain he had caused his brother with his words, though. "Now, are you gonna finish up so we can get movin' again? Or are you gonna sit here lollygaggin' the day through?"

Matt held his breath, a sense of humiliation coursing through him. "I'm done already, dammit," he snapped, tossing his tin plate in Buck's direction. He stood up and went to the horses and began saddling his.

Buck was mortified, and his heart sank down into his boots. Only moments before they were joshing much like in the old days. And moments later, Matt was acting like a wounded bear again. It made no sense to Buck. He started to apologize to his brother but stopped before any words came. There was, as far as he could tell, nothing to apologize for. And it wouldn't help Matt any, anyway.

With depression settling uncomfortably in on him, Buck set about cleaning up their breakfast mess, packing their meager supplies, and kicking some dirt over the fire. Matt was already mounted and waiting, looking impatient. Buck hurried to saddle his horse and mount up. Ducking until they were almost lying on their horses' necks, they rode out the doorway, into the drizzle of the gray day.

The sun broke through the clouds, which scattered before the assault, by midmorning. Wisps of steam corkscrewed upward from the wet grass and slick mud, as well as from their slickers and the horses.

They slept that night in the open, making a small, pungent fire of buffalo chips. Matt was surly and did not want to talk. Buck withdrew into himself, too, wondering about his brother.

Buck did not sleep well that night and was awake well before dawn. He lay in his blankets, thinking. He had decided, lying under the star-filled sky, that he would give Matt maybe another week to get back to something even close to his old self. If he didn't, Buck vowed, he would ride on by himself, leaving Matt to fight out his troubles alone.

Finally he got up and prepared breakfast. Only then did he rekindle the fire. He knew from long experience that such fuel as he was using might burn hot, but it burned fast, too. And he had no desire to sit and fiddle with a fire for hours on end.

Matt awoke and ate without a word, other than saying "Mornin'," when he first arose. Buck bit back his budding anger. He was already finished eating and had saddled his horse. When Matt finished and went to his mount, Buck hurriedly cleaned up. They rode out.

Near noon, with the sun riding hot and fierce overhead, Matt pulled into a copse of stunted cedar. With a look almost of excitement, Matt knelt by an old fire. Then he walked carefully around the camp, his eyes searching everything.

"What is it, Matt?" Buck asked. "Them?"

"Yep," Matt said sharply, adrenaline giving him a rush. "It hasn't rained here. They were here last night; moved out just this mornin'." His voice quivered in anticipation.

"Think we'll catch 'em today?"

"Yep," said Matt harshly as he pulled himself easily into his saddle. The gloom seemed to have lifted from him for the most part. He had a mission now, something to give him purpose. For the past day or so, he had not really believed they would find the Cherokees. Now he was certain they would—and soon.

He rode out, Buck following. They moved fairly slowly, as

Matt kept his eyes trained on the ground, following the trail of the Cherokees. He knew the mustangs' hooftracks better than he knew his own footprints. He pointed to a spot and said to Buck, "The old man shot a deer here. Him and Red Bird stopped just long enough to bleed it and throw it on the packhorse."

He moved on, going a little faster as anticipation pushed him. Later in the afternoon, with the sun beginning to fall, Matt stopped. Buck pulled alongside of him. "I smell a fire," Matt said.

"Think it's them?"

"It's likely. I ain't seen no other tracks."

"Where?"

Matt shrugged. "Dusk's too deep to tell. But it shouldn't be hard to find them now." His eyes gleamed in the fading light.

CHAPTER
★ 9 ★

Grace Red Bird awoke at the sound of a pistol being cocked. Her eyes popped open, wide with fear. All she could see was a glob of white face hovering low over her; and she felt the muzzle of a revolver brush her right cheekbone, just to the side of her nose.

John Long Ridge needed a little more prodding to have his slumber disturbed: A light kick in the side by Matt Ramsey did the trick. Long Ridge awoke much like his great-granddaughter had. "Mornin', Chief," Matt said without much humor. He was angry as could be and close to pulling the trigger.

Buck had known how Matt felt about losing his horse, and he was beginning to understand some of what Matt felt about himself since being wounded. Being afraid that his big brother might do something foolish, Buck had argued quietly but vehemently with Matt as they made their way slowly toward the camp.

"You can't just kill 'em, Matt," Buck had said, struggling to keep the volume of his voice down. A loud voice would carry far in the stillness here, he knew. But he was angry with, and even a little afraid of, the way Matt was acting.

Matt, for his part, wanted none of this argument. All he wanted to do was to sneak up on the camp, kill the two Cherokees, get his horse, and ride back toward his mustanging cabin over on the Trinity River. He and Buck had been gone only about three months, but it seemed to him like a lifetime. "Why not?" he asked in a low growl.

"Because," Buck said with resignation, as if he should not have to say something so obvious, "you're a Ramsey. And a Ramsey doesn't kill people in cold blood."

"It ain't cold blood," Matt insisted. "They're horse thieves."

"A Ramsey especially doesn't go killin' women and old men," Buck said with some finality.

"This Ramsey does."

"Bull."

Matt stopped and glared at Buck. "You sassin' me, boy?" he demanded.

Buck stared back evenly at him. Matt might be his big brother, but he no longer feared him. Buck was usually quiet and willing to take a back seat to Matt or Kyle. But when he believed in something, there was nothing that could sway him from it. He was, in that way, a Ramsey through and through.

"I'll do whatever's needed to stop you from committin' this foolishness, Matt," Buck said with quiet earnestness.

Matt continued staring, figuring to overwhelm Buck with his forcefulness. It didn't work. He saw a young man as strong-willed as himself—maybe more so, since Buck truly believed in what he was doing. Matt wanted to kill the Cherokees because he thought he should, not because he really believed it right. That gave Buck an edge. And it cut Matt to the heart again. Once more he was forced to back down, to accept a subservient role, as he saw it. He scowled, not wanting Buck to see his inner pain.

"I ought to whomp your butt good, boy," Matt snapped.

"If that'll stop you from killin' those Indians, I'll oblige you."

Matt was dejected. He was usually the strong one, the wise one. But he seemed to have lost all his roles of late. He nodded, trying desperately to battle down the sense of despair that threatened him. He succeeded, at least outwardly. "All right." He nodded. "I won't kill 'em." He felt he had to assert himself a little, though. "Right off. But the first time they try some stunt . . ."

"Fair enough," Buck said. He knew Matt was telling the truth. But Buck was still driven—by what, he did not know—to try to help the Cherokees. And he intended to do just that. But he figured he could talk Matt into it, too, but it would take awhile.

They had stopped a little bit earlier, figuring they were close enough for now. Matt estimated they were only half a mile from the Cherokees' camp, and he did not want to get any closer, risking the possibility of losing their prey. They dismounted, unsaddled, and cared for the horses. Then they sat down, backs against their saddles, both wishing they could have some coffee. But a fire was out of the question. They chewed a few biscuits they had left from that morning, washing the bone-dry meal down with water from their canteens.

Though plagued with his doubts, Matt once again showed sparks of his old self. He took out his Colt hogleg. With patience and care, he unloaded it, cleaned it, greased it with sperm oil, and reloaded it.

Buck, following his brother's lead, did the same with his Winchester. Neither man had really asked to go through life making his way with a gun. It was just the way things had turned out. Both had accepted that fact and lived with it. And because of that, they took good care of the tools of their trade.

"Why don't you catch a few winks, Matt," Buck suggested when they had finished their tasks.

"Think the old man needs some sleep, eh, boy?" Matt asked, stunning Buck with his acidness.

"No," Buck mumbled. "But you've been hurt, and . . . Well, with all the travelin' and . . ." He paused and sucked in a noisy breath. "The hell with it," he groused. "I was just offerin' to stand the watch if you wanted to shut your eyes a spell is all."

"No thanks." Matt was tired, but he was not about to give in to the feeling after Buck had just said such a thing. "Feel free to do so yourself, though."

"Reckon I will." Buck was too angry to really be able to sleep, but he slid down into his blankets, resting his head on his saddle. He pulled his hat down over his eyes and tried to relax.

He must've fallen asleep, Buck realized, when he shoved his hat up and the moon had shifted a considerable distance in the sky. He glanced over and thought Matt was sleeping. But he could not be sure in the darkness. Still, it was time they were up and moving. He stood up and thought for a minute, wondering whether he should wake Matt, since his brother had made no reaction when Buck had gotten to his feet.

Buck decided he would make a little noise: just enough to rouse Matt without alerting anyone who might be out there listening. This way Matt could pretend to have been awake the whole time. Buck stretched and yawned. He went into the brush to make water and sighed much more loudly that he normally would. He grinned when he heard a shifting from Matt behind him.

When he stepped back to his bedroll, Buck said loudly, "Well, thanks, Matt. I had me a good little nap." It was true, too: he felt refreshed.

"That's good." Matt stood up, rubbing his face and trying not to let Buck see how tired he was. He knew he had fallen asleep; he just hoped Buck had not known it. But the nap had done him little good.

"You set to leave?"

"Yep."

Each grabbed his rifle. They made sure their horses were securely tied to trees, and then they moved out on foot, trying not to stumble over rocks, fallen branches, brush, or roots. Branches whipped at them, tearing and scratching at their faces.

It took better than an hour and a half to cover the half-mile or so, but they finally made it to the small clearing amid the trees. Matt could hear the mustang snicker softly when it caught his scent, and he felt a grim satisfaction in that.

"Ready, Buck?" Matt asked in a whisper. Many of his doubts had fled. Action was almost upon him, and he focused on that.

"Yep."

"No use in waitin'."

They stepped into the tiny clearing, pistols drawn, rifles in their left hands.

"What're you gonna do with us?" asked John Long Ridge. His voice quavered, not so much from fear as from disappointment. He had traveled so many miles, rescued his great-granddaughter, and stolen horses for the trip. Now this.

"I'm of a mind to put a few slugs in your orn'ry hide, old man," Matt snapped. "But my brother here's got notions of bein' a doer of good deeds. Damn fool."

"So?" Long Ridge asked, still nervous. "What will you do with us?"

"Reckon we'll take you to the nearest town and turn you in for what you are—goddamn horse thieves."

"Better you should kill us now," Grace Red Bird said, also in English. She, too, was frightened. But she had been through too much to let this worry her overly much, and she managed to keep her voice sounding calm.

"Why?" Buck asked, surprised.

"You think them palefaces'll give us any kind of fair trial? Hoo, they'll hang us faster'n all get-out. And make a circus of it to boot. At least if you was to shoot us out here, it'd be over and done with, and our deaths wouldn't be for the amusement of such damned bloodthirsty paleskins."

"She's got a point, Matt," Buck said. Maybe this was his opportunity to convince his brother to help.

"Hell." Matt was angry again: partly because these Indians had stolen his horse, partly because he knew the woman was right. It smacked of cowardice to bring them to a town where they were certain to be hanged. Better to do it himself.

"You know what she says is true, Matt," Buck said earnestly. Still, he did not move the pistol, nor did he take his eyes off the girl.

Matt stood up, though still crouched over the old man, his finger itching. He was breathing heavily. Finally he very carefully straightened and eased the hammer of his pistol down. "Watch 'em both, Buck," he said.

It was light now as Matt moved toward the black mustang. He checked the horse over with infinite care, patting and reassuring the horse. The horse was a magnificent animal, taller than most prairie mustangs but with the barrel chest and endurance native to the breed. The horse could run like lightning when needed, or trot seemingly forever without flagging.

Matt gave the horse one last affectionate pat and strolled back to the little camp. "Y'all're both lucky," he drawled, "that you ain't mistreated my horse." He felt his strength returning to him, but he didn't know why. Nor did he really care. He was confident once again, and that gave him the strength to be magnanimous.

"Can you cook, girl?" he asked.

"Some," Red Bird admitted.

"Good. Buck, let 'em up, but keep your eyes on 'em. Get to cookin', girl. I know you got venison. We've got a spot of beans and flour left."

"Where?" Grace Red Bird asked as she stood up, Buck having stepped back.

"Never you mind. Just get the fire goin'. I'll fetch up the other stuff. Remember to keep your eye on 'em both, Buck." He headed back into the brush toward their new horses. As he did so, he grabbed Long Ridge's old rifle, grinning savagely back at the old Indian.

Red Bird rekindled the fire and put some venison on to roast. In a short while, Matt was back with the two horses, and he handed the food supplies to the Indian girl.

"I wondered how you caught up to us so fast," Long Ridge said with a wan smile. "Where'd you get the nags?"

Buck explained it quickly, and soon after, they ate. When the cooking pots had been cleaned up, and all were sitting around the fire, Long Ridge lit up an old clay pipe. "What now?" he asked.

"I ain't decided," Matt said laconically. "I'm still of a mind to shoot you. Damn, old man, you ought to know better'n to steal a man's horse."

Long Ridge shrugged. He was unembarrassed.

"Why'd you do it, Long Ridge?" Buck asked. "We said we'd help you."

"Didn't trust you," Long Ridge said simply, puffing out smoke. He belched and looked proud of it.

"Why?" Buck asked, startled.

"Put yourself in our place," Red Bird said.

Buck turned to look at her and was startled again by what he saw. She was not as beautiful, really, as Miss Eula Mae McFarrin, he decided. But there was something about the Cherokee girl that exerted a strong pull on him.

"I'd just been . . . well . . ." For the first time since he had known her, Buck saw Red Bird blush and look embarrassed. She stretched out her legs, which to Buck seemed mighty long for a short girl. And they were half-uncovered, too, what with the dress being so raggedy.

"Anyway," Red Bird said after a short pause, "it wasn't much of a good time for me, as you might well imagine. We finally got free and lost our horse, then walked for miles. Just as we were about to get yours, we was captured. I . . . I was afraid."

"Why?" Buck was a little discomfited now, and he seemed to be stuck on that word.

"Well, look at you two," Red Bird said, pointing to Buck and his brother. "Especially him." Her finger lingered accusingly on Matt. "He looks like some of the men with Cross. You do, too, Buck, except you're a mite young to be runnin' with that crowd."

"What do you mean, we look like Cross's men?" Buck demanded.

Matt sat with a tight smile on his face. He knew what the girl was talking about.

"You've got hard eyes," Red Bird said quietly. "You—and especially Matt—look like you've killed men before. You both have the taint of blood on you. It's not something you can do away with easily."

Buck looked ashamed, Matt rather amused. Long Ridge watched them both, as well as his great-granddaughter.

"I wish there was some way we could prove to you we ain't like those others," Buck said thoughtfully.

"There is," Matt said. All eyes turned toward him.

CHAPTER
★ 10 ★

They rode out in single file: Buck Ramsey leading the way, followed by John Long Ridge, then Grace Red Bird, who led the packhorse. Big Matt Ramsey brought up the rear.

"Why're you planning to ride behind everybody, eatin' dust?" Red Bird asked Matt.

Matt was riding the black mustang again, and for some reason, he felt better than he had in months. He grinned grimly. "Cause I ain't above shootin' you or Gramps there should you decide to ride off again."

"Oh." Red Bird shut up after that.

They had pulled out that morning, a day after Matt and Buck had caught up with the two Cherokees. Matt had ordered them to leave right away but was argued out of it. Matt was still a little tired anyway, and Red Bird had pulled him aside to tell him that Long Ridge needed at least a day's more rest. Matt had acquiesced.

They had all spent a day warily watching each other, none quite sure what any of the others would do. Matt napped a little, as did Buck, but never both at the same time. As darkness fell, and they all sat, full of venison and beans, Matt said quietly to his brother, "I'd be obliged if you was to spend the night up keepin' watch."

"What for?" Buck asked. He was not averse to the idea; he just wanted a reason.

"Make sure these two don't take off on us again. I don't mind none if they were to leave, but I'd be plumb angry they was to take the horses again." He grinned, looking almost like the Matt of old. "Besides, they need proof we ain't like Cross's bunch; I've told 'em we'll help 'em to show 'em we ain't, and, by God, I'm fixin' to see it through."

"You expect they'll try anything?"

Matt shrugged. "No tellin' what they'll do. I'd say not, though, if I was to guess. The old man looks about played out, and I don't reckon the girl'll leave him here. But . . . " He shrugged again. It was always best to be wary.

"All right. But you make sure you get some sleep."

"I will."

Buck was having a little trouble staying awake, since he had not gotten much sleep the night before. But he managed. He alternated his time between sitting with his back to a tree trunk and pacing around the camp.

Just after midnight, as best he could judge, he heard some rustling. He came alert. Then he saw Red Bird coming in his direction, which was away from the horses. That was a relief, anyway. He suddenly had the horrific thought that she was going to the bushes—and he was right in the way. But she stopped where he was sitting.

"Want some company?" she asked.

"Sure," he admitted nervously.

Red Bird sat down, smiling at him. Her teeth gleamed in the glare of the full moon. She was beautiful even close up like this. He thought back with a pleasurable flush to earlier in the evening. He had gone down to the river to bring up some water. He heard splashing and ducked into some brush, worried. He peered out, trying to locate the source of the sound. He finally did and gulped.

Grace Red Bird was standing knee-deep in the water, sort of sideways to him. She had her dress hiked up beyond her waist and was splashing water on her legs and beyond. Buck licked his lips, which were suddenly dry. He could not actually see anything except a great expanse of firm leg, but the images that boiled in his brain were vivid.

She was almost done, though, and within a minute she had dropped her dress to its full length. She scrubbed her face, then dunked her head into the river, trying to get some of the filth out of her hair. Then she was gone, wringing her long black hair in her hands as she walked.

Images of that scene rushed up and colored Buck's face as he sat across from her now. Her fingers touched his arm lightly. "I want to thank you, Buck," she said, with hesitancy in her voice.

"For what?" he asked, his face burning with embarrassment.

"For helpin' me and Grandfather. It wasn't for you, your brother would've shot us down."

"No he wouldn't have."

"Yes he would."

He started to argue, but she pressed soft fingers against his lips, sending a slight shock through him. She removed her fingers and replaced them with her lips.

Buck's eyes widened for a moment in shock, then closed as a pleasing warmth spread through him. Then Red Bird's mouth was gone from his, and he sat stunned, short of breath.

"I only know of one way to really thank a *man*," she said, emphasizing that last word, her voice sultry. She started to unbutton her shabby dress.

Buck gulped again. He was not innocent. He had been with women before, but this shook him, and he wasn't sure why. He tried to get his enraptured brain working, to think this through. Red Bird had her bodice undone and was shoving the top of her dress off her shoulders.

O Lord, Buck thought. He closed his eyes, shutting out the view of this beautiful, half-naked woman who was offering herself to him. The image of her lingered on the insides of his eyelids but then began to fade. That allowed his brain to begin functioning again. His eyes popped open. "Stop," he croaked.

It was Red Bird's turn to be startled. She stopped what she was doing, her hand resting lightly on the left shoulder of her dress. The right side was already shoved down, exposing her . . .

Buck had to close his eyes again and breathe deeply a few times to try to calm himself. His hormones were racing in his blood, bringing out a hot, flushed feeling.

"What?" asked Red Bird.

Buck opened his eyes and regretted it, since she was still sitting the way she had been. But he knew he had to keep his eyes open now, so she could see the earnestness in them. "This ain't right," he said softly, his throat thick with desire.

"Why?" she asked, truly surprised.

"Well . . ." He hesitated, figuring he was sounding like a fool. "Well, it just ain't."

"You ain't gettin' somethin' that ain't been had before, you know," Red Bird said bluntly. But there was sadness in her voice, too. "Not after what . . . Cross . . . and . . . the others . . . did to me."

"I know that." Buck sucked in air, trying to quiet the raging of his blood. "That still don't make this right, though." He groaned inwardly. Any man worth his salt would laugh him out of Texas for turning down a woman so beautiful and willing as this.

But he did believe this was wrong, this being so blatant about it all. And, worse, he thought it could be a trick of some sort. Once his brain had started to function a little, he realized what the nagging thought inside had been. He figured she could be doing this to distract his attention. Long Ridge could, this very minute, be heading for the horses. Buck could just picture the old Cherokee soothing the horses, then leading them away from camp a little bit. Then, after Buck had had his way with Red Bird, the Cherokee girl would slip away and disappear into the night—and to the waiting horses. Buck, sated from his experience, would be unwilling to chase after her, and they would get away, all because Red Bird was baring herself and offering herself and . . .

Best get your mind off THOSE things, Buck, he thought sternly.

Red Bird was still sitting there, one breast bare, the other nearly so. "You're sure?" she asked, her voice quavering.

"Yep." He was nowhere near that sure. But he had to be firm here.

"You mean you don't want me?" she asked, her lower lip beginning to tremble. Tears threatened to spill down her cheeks. She had conjured up the feeling of rejection, but now she began to realize that some relief—and wonder at this man's basic decency—flowed up within her and added to the sobbing.

"It ain't that I don't *want* you, Miss Red Bird," Buck said. *Lord, this is hard!*

"Then what?"

"I told you, this ain't right." He steeled himself and took another deep breath. "Please fix your dress. I can't talk with you sittin' there like that."

Red Bird smiled seductively but did as she was asked—though with agonizing slowness.

When Red Bird was covered again, Buck took another breath, somewhat in relief. "Look," he said, "I think you're very beautiful. Maybe the most beautiful girl I ever saw"—*and you saw a lot,* his brain screamed—"and I'd really like to . . . Well, you know." He waved a hand around vaguely.

He clamped his mouth shut and tried to work up some saliva. When he did, he said, "But just cause those . . . bastards . . . did what they did to you don't make you a loose woman. You don't have to offer yourself to a man this way to get him to like you."

Buck was certain his words were inadequate for what he wanted to say. But he just couldn't say it the way he thought he should. His mind and body were a jumble of exposed nerves and raging hormones.

But to Red Bird, they were more than adequate. It was the first time in her life that anyone considered her to be a whole person, one with thoughts and feelings. "I understand," she said. She still did not believe Buck Ramsey was this decent. No man could be. Or so had been her experience so far. Perhaps, she wondered, he was playing with her. She stared into his eyes, though, and realized that probably was not the case.

"You do?" Buck asked. He was torn between relief and regret. *Lord, how could I have passed up such an opportunity?* he wondered.

"Yep." She smiled. She did, too. She wasn't certain she liked it, but she thought she might be able to use it to her advantage, every bit as much as she could have his giving in to her.

Red Bird smiled again. "I like you, Buck Ramsey," she said.

"I should hope so," he responded fervently.

Red Bird stood up. "It still ain't too late to change your mind." She considered lifting her dress, to show him everything and see if that would get him to acquiesce. But she realized that such a thing would probably offend him more than soften him up. There would be plenty of time between their camp here on the Wichita River and her home on Sallisaw Creek for her to seduce this hard young man—if she thought it still necessary.

"I'm obliged for the offer, Miss Red Bird," Buck said, looking up at her, thinking—no, knowing, now—himself a fool for what he was doing. "But I'll pass," he added. *This time,* he thought.

Red Bird turned and headed back to the shabby blanket she used as a bed. She, too, was torn between regret and relief. She was glad she did not have to go through with it. But she did like Buck, and her naturally lusty soul craved to know what it would be like with a young man who was kind and considerate, rather than being taken by a pack of slavering animals. She shuddered as the memory of what had happened to her when she was a captive of Harlan Cross flashed through her. She felt close to vomiting for a moment.

Perhaps, she thought, she would take another stab at breaking through the stern exterior of Mr. Buck Ramsey. She smiled as she lay down. But it took her a long time to fall asleep.

On the trail, Matt kept a careful eye on the two Cherokees riding in front of him. He still did not trust them; especially the girl. The old man was probably too worn out to cause too much trouble. But the girl was full of vinegar and mischief. However, today she looked rather tired, and Matt wondered why. He had asked Buck about it this morning just before leaving. Buck had stammered and flamed pinkly on his face but finally said he did not know. That also left Matt wondering.

They rode slowly, not in much of a hurry. Matt wanted to spare the horses and give Long Ridge a chance to regain some vigor. Still, Matt was rather amazed at the old man, who was doing far better than Matt had expected him to after all the Cherokee had been through. Matt hoped to be doing as well at half Long Ridge's age.

And he wondered about Grace Red Bird. She was a fine-looking young woman. With a bath—a real bath; he knew the Cherokee had splashed herself off a few times in creeks and such—and a new dress and with her hair done up, she'd be a right pretty sight.

He tore his mind off those thoughts. He might be feeling some better about himself, but he still had doubts that lingered. He looked up at the sky. Clouds were bunching up there, and the wind had picked up some. With luck, the storm would pass them by, but he was not certain of that.

Buck called to him, and Matt hurried up to him. They walked their horses along. Buck did not want to point, so he just chucked his head in the right direction as he said quietly, "I see smoke out there, Matt. Seems to be a lot. Think it's a Comanche or Kiowa village or somethin'?"

Matt shrugged. He studied the smoke as they plodded onward. About an hour later, he said, "Lord, Buck, I think it's a town."

"You sure?" Buck asked, surprised.

"As much as I can be."

"You fixin' to stop there?"

"It'd be nice, I guess. Long Ridge and Red Bird ain't fitted out for a storm. And I suppose it'd be nice sleepin' in a bed."

Buck nodded.

CHAPTER
11

Calico, Texas, was a small place and didn't look like much. But it had a real hotel and a real general store, among other things, and that was a relief to the weary travelers.

The town was a jumble of small streets and alleys off the main thoroughfare, which was a meandering road in itself. Businesses and abodes of all sorts—wood, sod, stone, adobe—were scattered all over the place, haphazardly put up wherever the owner decided he would like it. There was no rhyme or reason to the scheme of the town. A few buildings were substantial and well-constructed of adobe or stone, but most of the buildings looked as if a good wind would flatten them.

Clothes flapped in the breeze from poles or makeshift clotheslines; and tumbleweeds blew along the streets, mingling with the garbage. With the leaden gray sky, it presented a dismal picture all and all. But the travelers did not mind. Matt Ramsey had decided that as soon as they had seen the town they would spend the night there. A storm was brewing, and even if it wasn't a bad one, half the group was ill-prepared to face it. He and Buck had their slickers and their hats, which would keep the worst of the rain off them. But John Long Ridge and Grace Red Bird had nothing but the clothes they wore and a thin blanket each.

September was here, and Matt Ramsey could feel it in the air.

A chill had come with the clouds, and the nights of late were quite cool. Though the days were still plagued by searing heat, he knew winter was on its way.

Matt had done a heap of thinking on the trail that day. He felt mostly like his old self, and that pleased him. Sure, he acknowledged, there were twinges of pain—both mentally and physically—but that did not seem to matter any more. He could feel the sense of helplessness lurking not far below the surface, and he vowed to keep it under control.

He wondered frequently during the slow, plodding travel just what had made him agree to help these two horse-stealing Indians. Probably the old Ramsey pride, he thought more than once. Long Ridge and Red Bird had, in a sense, challenged him. By letting it be known that they considered him much like Cross's bunch, he felt stricken by pride and his Scottish stubborn streak. He would, he told himself, show them that he was not like Harlan Cross.

Of course, he was reluctant to admit, even to himself, that he was mostly to blame for the two Cherokees feeling the way they did. Had he not been so surly and wrapped up in his own conjured-up troubles, he would not have treated the Indians so poorly in the first place.

Buck's constant arguing—and lecturing—also helped him grow back to what he should be. Buck could never know the shame Matt had felt at the younger Ramsey's joyous ribbing of Matt— of poking fun when Matt had wrestled with Red Bird and almost lost; and other times. But Matt knew, deep in his gut, that all this was really his own problem, not Buck's. The younger Ramsey was actually just doing what he always did, joshing and jesting with his older brother. If Matt couldn't take it, well, Buck couldn't be blamed for that, even if he couldn't see the torment his brother felt.

In a way, Matt felt challenged by Buck, too. He felt challenged, mentally, to become the Matt Ramsey he really was, just to show his brother that all was right.

But he felt challenged physically, too. Because of his wound, Matt had not been as sharp of late as he normally was, so Buck had—naturally, as was right, Matt knew—taken over the harder tasks. He had handled them—and himself—well, Buck had. And Matt was secretly proud of Buck because of that. He would not, however, let his brother know how he felt.

The fight with the stage robbers had done a lot to make Matt feel better. Not that he felt better after having been forced, more or less, to kill a man, but because he had handled himself with at least some of the flair and competence of old.

Finding and winning back his black mustang again had almost completed the process of rehabilitation. He felt almost—not quite, but almost—a whole man once again. And it was with strength and authority that he announced they would head for the town and spend the night there.

Buck had looked ready to argue about the decision. He had had enough of small towns like this after his experience in Justice. Then he saw the fire of life in Matt's eye. He grinned and nodded. "All right, Matt," he said, happy to seemingly have his brother back.

The motley group stopped in front of MacGregor's Hotel and dismounted wearily. "Stay here with these two, Buck," Matt said. "I'll see about gettin' us a room."

"Might not be easy, Matt." Buck pointed to a sign that hung just to the right of the glass-paned double doors of the hotel.

The badly painted sign, with its crooked, poorly executed letters in bright yellow, read:

NO
NIGGERS
GREASERS
REDSKINS

"I can sense the warmth of fellowship already," Matt said sarcastically. He straightened his broad shoulders and winked at Buck. "Can't hurt to try, though, can it?" He crossed the small wood sidewalk and entered the hotel.

A short, rotund man stood puffing behind the small desk, a set of open boxes behind him. He was sweating heavily, and his heavy breathing made his cheeks flap. "Yessir, what can I do for you?" the fat man asked, his brogue thick. "Angus MacGregor at your service."

"Need a room," Matt said pleasantly.

"You alone?"

"Nope. Got my brother and two friends with me."

"Two rooms?" The man's eyes glittered greedily.

"One ought to do," Matt said blandly. "Got to watch your pennies, you know."

"Aye." MacGregor nodded sagely. "The restaurant next door is mine. Meals are fifty cents. It opens at six. The room'll cost you a buck and a half. I don't want no loud noise, no liquor, no gunplay. No women, either." MacGregor winked at this last restriction.

Matt nodded and scratched his name in the register. He handed over some coins.

"By the way, where're the others?"

"Outside. There a livery in town?"

"Other end of town, along the river." MacGregor tried to see past Ramsey outside, hoping to catch a glimpse of Matt's companions, but he couldn't.

"Thanks," said Matt with a sharp nod. "We'll be back directly." He turned, not allowing MacGregor to say—or see—anything much, and walked outside.

"He say anything about Long Ridge and Red Bird?" Buck asked.

"He don't know about 'em yet," Matt said with a grin. "I reckon he'll be some put out when he learns of it, though." He shrugged, unconcerned about what the fat old Scotsman would have to say about it. "Let's go." He knew MacGregor would be edging up to the door to get a look, so Matt told Long Ridge and Red Bird to walk ahead of him and Buck, keeping the two Cherokees blocked off from the prying eyes of the innkeeper.

The Ramseys were no strangers to having people stare at them. Neither were the Cherokees, for that matter. The four walked their horses slowly toward the livery, conscious of the glares cast in their direction. Matt and Buck were wary, alert, ready for trouble. Long Ridge and Red Bird looked frightened by the hate that flowed over them in torrents from the eyes of the townspeople.

But no one bothered them during their seemingly endless journey across the dismal little town. The man who ran the livery did not look happy at the darker two of his four new customers, but he took their business.

"I'd be obliged if these animals were to get a little special care," Matt said sternly.

The look on Matt's face let the liveryman know that argument would be foolish, unsuccessful, and possibly fatal if pushed beyond a certain limit.

"Yessir," the man said.

The four visitors to the town headed back up the street, in the general direction of the general store, once again braving the stares of a generally hostile citizenry. They strode boldly into Carter and Hall's Mercantile.

Two men in white shirts, with garters on their sleeves and wearing green eyeshades, waited on customers—a cowboy in the hat section and two middle-aged matrons in an area dominated by bolts of cloth. Both shopkeepers looked up when the four entered.

"Get them goddamn redskins outta my store," the taller and older of the two said, glaring at them. He wore gold spectacles and had a thin, wilted mustache. A patch of bald pate stuck up out of the hole behind the eyeshade.

"What's that?" Matt asked innocently.

The shopkeeper turned to the women he was helping and said, "Excuse my blunt language, ladies." He faced the Ramseys and the Cherokees again. "I said, boy, get them goddamn red savages out of my store." He pointed a long, thin accusatory finger toward the small group.

"That's a damn poor attitude for a shopkeeper to have, friend."

"I don't give a horse's ass," the man growled, as if he expected to inspire fear in someone. "There's a sign plain as the day right outside that says I don't want no goddamn redskin savages in here. I mean it, too."

"He givin' you trouble, Mr. Hall?" said the cowboy, who was trying on a hat. He wore a cotton shirt, wool pants, and leather chaps. A Remington hung at his left hip.

"Ain't sure yet, Cal. But I expect he'll do like I say."

Matt's face hardened. He looked at the other store man and whispered to his brother, "Keep your eye on that cowpoke, Buck." He glared at the shopkeeper next to the cowboy and said quietly, but with deadly menace, "If I was you, mister, I'd come up from behind that counter slow and smooth, 'less you want another bellybutton."

He had made no move toward his Colt, but he didn't need to. The storekeeper straightened stiffly.

"You got somethin' else you'd like to say?" Matt addressed the cowboy.

"No, sir," was the reply. The cowpoke was torn between anger and fear. But he had enough sense to know better than to try throwing down against two guns wielded by men like these. With one, he might have a chance; but not two.

"Now," Matt said calmly, turning back to Hall, "did you have somethin' you wanted to say to me?"

"We don't allow no goddamn—" He froze and slapped his mouth shut at the hard look on Matt's face. "We don't allow no Indians in here, mister. It's the same at most places in town." He let it be known that any business that would allow such a thing was not worth mentioning in polite society.

"Why not?"

The man shrugged. "Bad for business." He was not embarrassed by it; he was proud, in fact.

"Bullshit." Matt glanced around the store. He was used to such things, growing up when and where he had. But he never agreed with it, nor took kindly to it.

"It's all right, Mr. Ramsey," John Long Ridge said softly. "We'll wait outside." The old warrior was also used to such treatment and had learned his place years before. It did not even humiliate him any longer.

Matt knew it would be best to have the two Cherokees wait outside, but he was in a stubborn mood. "You know, mister," he said to Hall, "you'd get a lot further with folks was you to change your ways some. I might've missed your sign outside. All you had to do was ask nice and I would've had my friends here wait outside." It wasn't true. He would have reacted in the same way even if the store owner had been pleasant about it. Still, Hall did not know that.

"That's neither here nor there," the man blustered.

"Reckon it is," Matt agreed, his visage hard. He sighed. "You're lucky you're the only general store in these parts. I'd as soon take my business somewhere else, but there ain't no place else."

Hall began to grin rudely in victory. But the smile died when Matt added, "And I don't really feel like killin' anybody else today. I reckon two or three a day's enough for any man. Eh, Buck?"

"Hell, Matt, let me shoot one of 'em. I only got one today." Buck was rather proud of his acting.

"Don't get spoiled on me now, boy. Mr. Long Ridge," he said politely over his shoulder, "will you escort Miss Red Bird outside and wait for us there?"

"Yes, sir," said Long Ridge with great dignity.

"Go with 'em, Buck."

"Why?" Buck asked, startled. "They ain't gonna run away."

"I ain't worried about 'em runnin'," Matt said quietly. "What I am worried about, though, is that some of the good citizens of Calico might decide to do somethin' foolish."

"But . . ." Buck jerked his head in the cowboy's direction.

"Ain't you got some other business you could tend to?" Matt said in the cowboy's direction.

The cowhand gulped and then nodded. He hurried outside.

"These others ain't gonna give me no trouble, Buck. Are you, boys?"

Carter and Hall shook their heads.

"As I thought. Go on now, Buck. Long Ridge and Red Bird'll be needin' you to watch over 'em. I don't trust a one of these people in this goddamn town. Just make sure you keep your eyes peeled and your Winchester ready."

"Yes, sir," Buck muttered. But he felt good. It was nice to have Matt back, he thought, as he stepped outside with the two Cherokees.

Inside, Matt felt pretty good himself. He was in charge again, with only a few lingering doubts still crowding into the back of his mind. "Now, sirs," he said almost pleasantly, "what we need is this." He began to feel more comfortable as he ran off his list.

CHAPTER
★ 12 ★

Buck could sense trouble coming; he could feel it deep down in his young bones. He didn't know when it would happen or where it would come from. He only knew it would happen.

Because of that, he was even more alert than usual, his eyes scanning the hostile faces that passed by; the windows of the buildings across the way; the carriages and wagons that clattered and rattled up and down Calico's dusty main street.

John Long Ridge and Grace Red Bird were nervous and had backed up as near to the wall of Carter and Hall's Mercantile as they could get without actually blending into the rough wood planking.

Buck wanted to talk a little with Long Ridge, more so with Red Bird. But he dared not lose his concentration. Buck Ramsey was not a man who let hardships in life lay too heavily on him, but he had learned early—and well—that to be too lax where danger was threatening meant death, which could come fast and hard.

So he concentrated on watching everyone who passed, to be aware of every window and door. He showed no outward signs of his nervousness; he just looked stern and determined.

Ten tense minutes later, Matt stepped out of the store carrying a box loaded with supplies. Buck felt a flash of relief. Behind Matt came Carter and then Hall, each carrying a burlap sack. With distaste, each storekeeper held the sack out toward one of the

Cherokees. Long Ridge, still worried, smiled nonetheless when he took the sack. Red Bird looked like she was about ready to spit on Hall when she took the other bag. But she didn't.

"I'm obliged for your help, boys," Matt said facetiously to the two shop owners. Carrying the box in his left arm and resting it on his hip, Matt turned and led the way across the street toward the hotel.

Long Ridge and Red Bird followed, walking side by side, their heads held high despite their fear, which was a palpable thing for them. Buck brought up the rear, cradling his rifle in his left hand, where it was easily accessible. He had his and Matt's saddlebags slung over his left shoulder.

The group endured a considerable amount of hostility during the short walk but encountered no outright resistance or even harassment. They strode dauntlessly into MacGregor's Hotel.

"Hold it right there," MacGregor ordered. His fat face was redder than usual, and he was soaked in sweat. He held a scattergun in trembling hands.

Matt stopped and opened his eyes wide in innocent wonder. The large orbs held MacGregor's attention, even as Matt's right hand edged toward his Colt. He was getting tired of such foolish people. "There a problem, Mr. MacGregor?" he asked calmly.

"Aye, laddie, I'd say there was." His brogue seemed even more prominent than it had been earlier.

"And what's that?"

"Ye dinna tell me your friends were savages, Mr. Ramsey." He almost "tsked" him in annoyance and disappointment.

"Didn't think it mattered," Matt said blandly.

"Ye saw the sign outside yon door, laddie. It was put there for a purpose, as ye might imagine. I dinna put it there to be ignored by the likes of ye."

Matt looked shocked and hurt. "Ye canna tell me, Mr. MacGregor," he said, rolling his Rs as much as MacGregor did and adopting as heavy a brogue as the innkeeper, "that a good Scotsman such as yourself would let the small-minded people in such a town as Calico dictate how you'd be carryin' on your business."

"Well . . ." MacGregor said slowly, his convictions wavering just a little.

"Unless," Matt said, with a sharper bite to his tone, "ye really don't have the blood of a true Highlander runnin' through your veins. Ye canna tell me you're not really a Scotsman at all, mon!" He looked horrified at the thought.

"I should say not, sir," MacGregor growled, offended.

"I have my doubts that those're true words," Matt allowed sternly. "No true Scot would allow himself to be ruled in such a fashion. 'Tis somethin' I learned from a real Scotsman: my father, Samuel Ramsey."

MacGregor looked doubtful. "But you dunna have to live in this godforsaken place, Mr. Ramsey." He shook his head, his flabby cheeks swaying. "'Tis hard on business to accept such folk as those"—he pointed at Long Ridge and Red Bird—"at my inn."

Matt shrugged. "We'll be gone come mornin'. All this'll be forgotten in a couple days."

"They will stay here, Angus," a woman said. A short and quite stout female entered the small lobby from a room in the back, the MacGregors' personal quarters. "These Indians have done nothing against us."

"But Mary—" MacGregor started.

"Och, mon, stop your whimperin'. I dinna marry such a weaklin' man that'd be worried o'er every little thing the folks might say aboot him."

Mary MacGregor was nearly as rotund as her husband. She must have been pretty, though, when she was younger, Matt thought as he looked at her. Her once red hair was now dulled by the heavy lace work of gray, and her fleshy cheeks and double chins wobbled when she talked.

"But Mary," MacGregor started again, trying for a semblance of respect.

It was as if she did not even hear him. "And put that gun away before someone gets hurt."

"But that's the idea, lassie," MacGregor snapped, trying to reassert himself.

"Aye, I guess it is, sir. But just who are ye plannin' to shoot, eh? The old man? The girl, perhaps?"

"Well . . ."

"They're the savages ye're so afraid of? Are they the ones ye'll shoot?"

"No, I thought . . ."

"If you thought anything at all, Angus MacGregor, ye'd not be standin' here with that foolish gun in your hand." She glared at her husband. "But if ye're gonna shoot someone," she added after a moment's pause, "I'd suggest ye try gettin' the big, dark-haired laddie first." She grinned at Matt. "But, since by doin' that, ye'll be killed for certain by yon fair lad, I hope to the Sweet Lord that ye've left me well off."

"Och, Mary," MacGregor snapped, "ye are a trial and a tribulation to a man. I dunna ken why I e'er married ye."

"Cause ye had sense once," Mary said without hesitation. "But it appears ye've lost it o'er the years, Mr. MacGregor."

MacGregor sighed, knowing he was beaten. When Mary started calling him *Mister* MacGregor, he knew his cause was lost. With a sad shake of his head, MacGregor stashed the shotgun under the counter. "Don't e'er get married, Mr. Ramsey," he said in Matt's direction. "The comforts of the marriage bed are not worth the grief your woman'll give ye."

Mary MacGregor grinned widely. "The bloody sun in this infernal land has finally made him daft, Mr. Ramsey," she said with a laugh. "Aye, it has. Ye'll have to be excusin' him and his lack of civility because of that."

"Yes'm," Matt said with a smile.

"I'll take ye to your rooms now." Mary led the way up the stairs to the second floor and down a hallway to a room in the southwest corner. "It'll let you keep an eye on the main street and the alley next door," she said as she opened the door. She grew somber. "And make no mistake, laddie, trouble's a waitin' on ye and your kith and kin."

Matt nodded and entered. The room was small, with one rickety wooden bed covered by a fine quilt. There was a fat chair near one window and on the opposite side a small table on which sat a pitcher and basin. A chamber pot was under the table. Several coal-oil lamps were tacked to the walls. The room was clean, if not very fancy, and there was sufficient floor space.

Mary left, and Buck kicked the door shut behind her. They all put their packages on the bed. Then, ill at ease, they looked at their surroundings, no one quite knowing what to say.

Matt turned, grinning mischievously. "Well, let's go on back to the store," he said with a chuckle.

"What?" Buck asked, surprised and worried. "What for?"

"Long Ridge and Red Bird need some new duds. We ain't gonna find 'em here."

"We don't need nothin'," Red Bird said sharply. She appeared angry, but she was really afraid. She just hoped it didn't show to the others.

Matt's face clouded over in determination. "Maybe you've been beat down by life enough that you'll accept such things as these people've been handin' out here," he said harshly. "But I'll be damned if I'll stand for such nonsense. I didn't let the damn blue bellies break me in Vicksburg, and I sure as hell ain't gonna let a bunch of peckerwood Texans do so."

Buck almost cheered. Now, this was the Matt he knew!

"Come on, let's go," Matt said, making an order of it. He headed for the door.

Red Bird followed, fright beginning to get the better of her. Long Ridge tried mostly successfully to stifle a grin. Matt would have made one heck of a warrior, Long Ridge thought. Buck shut the door behind them.

They marched across the street and strode brazenly into Carter and Hall's. Both store owners looked near to falling over from the dose of apoplexy that had transfixed them.

"What'n hell're you four doin' back in here?" Hall demanded in a squawking voice.

"Forgot some things," Matt said gleefully, enjoying himself for the first time in months.

"Well, go and get 'em someplace else," Carter said in angry indignation.

"Now, you know damn well there's no place else to go," Matt said simply.

"What do you want?" Hall growled.

"Don't cozy up to 'em, Bill," Carter snapped.

"We want to be shed of 'em," said Hall. "The quicker we wait on 'em, the quicker we'll get 'em the hell out—for good."

"Your partner's a smart man, Carter," Matt said. "You ought to heed him more often." He paused. "All we need're some clothes for our two friends. For us, too, come to think about it."

It did not take long to pick out what was needed: two pairs of pants and two shirts each for the men; two dresses, a bonnet, and a pair of shoes for Red Bird; a new top hat for Long Ridge; a slicker and heavier blankets for the two Cherokees.

Matt paid from his dwindling supply of cash. "See, Carter," he said as he pocketed his change, "it didn't take long, now did it?"

Each picked up a paper-wrapped package of clothing, and then they all headed for the door, Matt again leading.

As he reached for the knob, Matt called softly, "Buck."

The younger Ramsey moved up to be next to his brother. "Trouble's a brewin', I think," Matt said.

Buck looked outside through the windows in the door. "We walk out?" he asked. "Or do we make a stand here, inside?"

"I doubt we'd find much protection in here," Matt said grimly. "Not as long as Carter's got that scattergun back there."

"Let's go, then."

"Here, take this, Long Ridge," Matt said, handing his package to the Cherokee, while Buck handed his to Red Bird. "Ready, Buck?" Matt asked.

"I reckon."

Matt yanked open the door and stepped out, with Buck right behind him. Matt stopped, and the younger Ramsey moved up alongside his brother. The Cherokees came out of the store tentatively.

Cal, the cowboy who had been in the store earlier, stood in the street, just off the wood sidewalk, waiting for them. He had four companions with him. "I reckon it's time you was taught a lesson, mister," Cal said. He stood rocking on his heels, his thumbs hooked into his gunbelt, feeling quite the cock of the walk.

"What kind of lesson?" Matt asked, smirking.

"Gawd, you're a stupid one, ain't you," Cal said with a low chuckle of derision. He shook his head in wonder. "Don't even know what I'm talkin' about when you're standin' there with a couple of goddamn redskins. Lord, it's gonna take a pile of learnin' for you to get anything through your thick head. Ain't that right, boys?"

A chorus of affirmatives rose up from the small knot of cowhands behind him.

"It's amazin', ain't it, Buck," Matt said with a lightness that belied his anger, "how folks who're dumber'n a can o' lard keep wantin' to teach smarter folks all kinds of things."

"Hard to believe, Matt," Buck agreed.

Cal's face darkened as he tried to comprehend how he had lost the advantage here. "Damned, stupid, Injin-lovin' son of . . ."

"Watch your tongue, boy," Matt said, the humor wiped from his face. "Unless you'd rather lose it."

"Damn you," Cal shouted. He launched himself at Matt.

CHAPTER
13

Matt shifted to his right two steps and clubbed Cal down with his big right fist as the cowboy steamed forward. Cal grunted as Matt's knuckles splatted against his flesh, and he stumbled a few more steps before falling on his face. His head barely missed the wall of Carter and Hall's store.

Cal tried to get up, but Long Ridge hurriedly stepped up and kicked him in the side of the head. Cal moaned softly and sank onto the sidewalk.

The four other cowboys charged en masse, heading toward the big, dark-haired man, seemingly having forgotten Buck.

The younger Ramsey dropped his Winchester on the sidewalk and flung himself at the charging cowpokes, bowling over three of them.

They all went down in a sprawl of arms and legs, flopping and twisting in the dirt. Buck had the fleeting—and totally lunatic—thought that he was glad he had not put his new clothes on if he was going to be rolling around the dusty, manure-splattered streets of Calico.

He scrambled up and was knocked straight back down again by a flying fist that Buck did not even see. He grunted softly and rolled a few times, hoping to gain room enough to stand. If he could do that, he figured he would be all right.

Matt was caught by the fourth cowboy, who slammed a shoulder into his midsection, driving him backward. Matt's breath popped out with a rush when his back smashed hard against the wall of the store. Pain jabbed its way like a fiery-hot poker deep into his chest, and Matt gasped with the sudden sharpness of it. He whipped both balled fists outward and then flashed them back in toward the cowhand. His fists cracked against the cowboy's ears.

The cowpoke's head rang with the explosion of air against his eardrums, and he roared at the shock of pain. He staggered backward, clapping his hands over the injured organs. His heel caught on the edge of the wood sidewalk, and he teetered a moment, before slipping off backward. Unable to catch himself, he landed almost flat on his back, moaning with the impact.

"Go get 'em, Buck!" Matt roared with a vicious grin, watching his brother as he faced the three other cowboys. He relaxed just a little. If there was fighting like this to be done, it was better to let Buck handle it. Matt might be bigger, and even stronger, but when it came to a scrap like this—a knock-down, dragout, ear-biting, eye-gouging free-for-all—well, Buck was the one for it. Matt could hold his own in such a fracas when the need came, but Buck, for some reason, was far more adept at such things.

Matt also had a spark of fear lingering in the back of his mind. The crash into the wall had sent a lancing blade of pain through his chest where he had been wounded. All along Matt had worried that he was not up to full strength, that any overly strenuous activity would lay him low. That fear lingered, though he was feeling a mite better. The ache in his chest had abated, and he felt strong and certain of himself. Still, there was a kernel of doubt that had buried itself so deep into his brain in the past two months that it was almost impossible to shake.

So Matt decided he would stand here and watch Buck, seeing how the younger Ramsey did. He could also wade in should it seem Buck was not doing well.

Buck had gotten up after catching that one fist in the face. And Lord, was he fighting mad about it, too. He swiped a hand across his jaw, leaving a trail of dirt. Out of the corner of his eye, he saw Matt get slammed into the wall of Carter and Hall's store, and he figured Matt was out of this fight.

One of the cowboys laughed at him. "Looks like you're all alone, sonny," he said.

The cowpoke was forty years old if he was a day. The stubble on his face was specked with white, and his hair was quite thin and mostly gray. He wore a crusty cotton shirt, faded blue jeans, and cracked leather batwing chaps. His boots were covered with manure. He was not tall, but he was lean and had the look of a rabid whippet dog about him.

Buck sneered at him. "That ain't so bad, I reckon, if all I'm facin' is three fallin'-down drunks like you and those other two oafs."

The other two were an unlikely pair. One was short and plump, with the face of a bulldog, all wrinkled up and pushed in. He wore wool pants that were patched considerably and above them only the filthy top of a pair of longjohns.

The other was a foot and a half taller and far skinnier, and he appeared to have none of his joints hooked up just right. His pants ended several inches above the ankles and his shirt sleeves were the same above his wrists.

"You talk mighty big for a boy about to get his butt stomped into the dirt," the first said easily.

"Oh," Buck said, feigning surprise, "you want to fight? Hell, I thought you were sent by the town quiltin' society come to flap your gums till I fell down dead."

The cowboy was about to retort when he was interrupted by a bellow of pain from one of his companions. He turned in shock to see the one who had rammed into Matt, roaring and holding his ears. He fell off the sidewalk and lay still, not unconscious but trying to escape the pain of his busted ears.

"What's it gonna be, pal?" Buck asked the cowboy. He let an insolent sneer creep across his face.

"You son of a bitch," the cowboy snorted. He and his two companions charged at Buck.

Buck never knew exactly how or what he did in a brawl like this; he just did it. He kicked and bit and scratched and punched. He bellowed and roared and spit. He felt satisfaction each time a fist or knee or elbow connected with flesh or bone, and he enjoyed the howls of pain and enraged curses he brought forth.

Time lost all meaning and connection with reality. One minute he was a whirling dervish of arms and legs; the next Matt was standing behind him, strong arms wrapped around him in a friendly but firm bear hug. "Whoa, Buck," he said with a chuckle. "I think these boys've done enough damage to you."

Buck calmed down and came back to his senses. He looked around. The three cowboys who had attacked him were lying in the dirt in various stages of bleeding, moaning, or both. None looked ready to stir up any more trouble.

"I couldn't have done it without your help, big brother," Buck said sarcastically. He bent over, resting his hands on his knees, and puffed to regain his breath.

Matt laughed. It was a good sound for Buck to hear, and one long overdue, Buck thought. "I figured I could be the most help if I stayed out of your way. Hell, I've seen you in fights like this before. I was to wade in and try to help, I'd only wind up gettin' the stuffin' knocked out of me. I got no desire to take a siesta out here in the street alongside those other boys."

"I don't know why," Buck allowed, still bent over and breathing heavily. "A man your age needs all the sleep he can get."

"Why you little—"

He stopped and whirled as he heard John Long Ridge yell, "Matt! Buck!"

Matt saw the Indian's outstretched arm. He continued spinning, drawing out his Colt with smooth efficiency.

At the same time, Buck snapped upright as his Winchester came sailing through the air from Long Ridge. Just as he grabbed it, Matt shoved him aside and fired the Colt.

Buck looked up to see Cal get smacked back up against the store's wall and begin to slide down it. He left a trail of blood on the wall as his pistol discharged harmlessly into the sidewalk and then fell from lifeless fingers.

Buck was not thinking consciously during all this. He noted it with a now-practiced eye. He simply took in the fact that the cowboy who had plowed into his brother earlier was up and aiming his Colt at Matt. Buck snapped a round into the Winchester's chamber and fired from the hip.

The bullet only winged the cowpoke in the left arm. But it threw the man's aim off, and his shot ended up in the side of a wagon down the street. Buck yanked the lever on his rifle and fired more carefully this time. The bullet burrowed into the cowboy's stomach, knocking him off his feet. He wasn't dead, but he would be causing no more trouble.

As Buck fired at the cowpoke, Matt spun until his back was to the store—and the armed man. He had no fear of being shot; not when Buck was there with his Winchester. But he wanted to protect their rear in case the beaten-up cowboys—or anyone else, for that matter—wanted to try something.

The three cowhands were still on the ground, though showing

some signs that they would be ambulatory soon. A few horrified townfolk stood around gawking, while others had rushed for safety. Matt heard Buck's Winchester and then the falling body, and he nodded mentally.

"Whether you boys can stand or not," Matt said harshly, "pull your pieces out slow and easy and toss 'em aside. Now!"

The one with the loose joints had managed to unfold himself, and he stood up. He eased out his pistol and tossed it aside. He had no desire to get himself killed at the hands of these crazy men. His friend Cal had just wanted him and the others to throw a scare into a couple of Indian lovers. That was all.

His two companions felt about the same. Both were still on the ground, the whippet sitting, the bulldog on hands and knees. Each pulled his pistol and threw it after the other.

Matt called behind him, "Everything all right, Buck?"

"Yep," Buck said tightly.

"Keep on your toes." Matt slid his Colt away. He walked warily to the three pistols in the dirt. Keeping his eyes on the three men, he bent his knees and sank. He scrabbled around in the dirt with his left hand until he found a pistol. Without looking at it, he unloaded it and tossed it in the general direction of the three cowboys. He did the same with the other two.

Rising slowly, he said, "Unless you boys want to join your cronies down to the undertaker's, I'd recommend you make yourselves scarce."

They needed no further encouragement. All three skedaddled down the street as fast as their battered bodies could take them.

Matt watched them for a moment. He turned slowly, sighing with regret. He was not a man who took to killing lightly, and it always bothered him when it happened. And, as far as he was concerned, it had happened too often of late.

"Reckon we ought to do somethin' with these two, Matt?" Buck had his rifle up on his shoulder, the lever skyward. It would be in firing position in the blink of an eye, should it be needed.

"Like what?" Matt asked, not much caring. "They ain't no kin of mine."

Buck shrugged. He took a look around, his eyes serene but missing nothing. "I expect the good folks of Calico'll see to 'em," Matt said.

"I expect." Buck stepped up onto the sidewalk. "I'm much obliged, Mr. Long Ridge," he said. "We would've been in poor straits if you hadn't warned us."

Long Ridge beamed proudly but said quietly, "I could do nothin' else." Red Bird nodded.

"Come on, Buck," Matt said. "Best gather up these packages and get back to the hotel. I expect the law'll be here any time now." He looked around, concerned. "I'm surprised they ain't been here already."

"Probably scared of the two *loco* Injin lovers," Buck said, forcing out an unauthentic chuckle.

"I reckon." He sighed and bent to pick up his package, which Long Ridge had dropped to toss Buck his Winchester. The others each grabbed a bundle, and they headed slowly toward the hotel.

They encountered fewer hostile glances this time, mostly because they encountered fewer people. But it was still an uneasy walk, with Buck and Matt trying to watch everything and everywhere at once. The trek seemed interminable.

As they stepped up onto the sidewalk, Buck stopped and pointed with his rifle. "Look," he said, wonder filling his voice.

"What?" Matt asked. His mind was elsewhere.

"The sign. The damn sign's gone." His voice was almost filled with awe.

The others looked. Sure enough, where the offensive painted board had hung there was now just hotel wall—less stained than the whitewash surrounding the rectangular space.

"Maybe this wasn't all bad, after all," Matt said as he opened the door to the hotel.

MacGregor was still behind his counter, still sweating. But he was grinning widely. "Evenin', laddies," he said rather pleasantly. "And lass, of course."

"Mr. MacGregor," the four answered.

"Have ye noticed the change to the hotel?" he asked.

"Aye," Matt answered, not quite mocking the innkeeper.

"Makes it a better place, don't you think?"

"I'd say so," Buck allowed.

MacGregor nodded, pleased. "Well, ye folks go to your room now. Ye'll need your rest after your . . . endeavors today. Your sleep'll not be disturbed. Me and Mrs. MacGregor will see to that."

"I'd be obliged for a good night's sleep," Matt said honestly. He led the others upstairs.

CHAPTER
⋆ 14 ⋆

The small group was plumb glad to leave the wretched little town of Calico behind as they rode out the next morning. They had been rather tense for a while, waiting for the law to show up.

The sheriff did, and the small group huddled around the railing at the top of the stairs and listened in as the lawman was turned away by an adamant Angus MacGregor and his formidable wife, Mary. The sheriff—and two seemingly self-appointed deputies—stomped off, muttering low curses and threats of how the MacGregors were finished in this town.

Matt grinned as he led his brother and friends back to their room. "Friendly cuss, ain't he?" he said with a chuckle.

They relaxed in the room for a while, tending to their own affairs. The two Cherokees chatted quietly in their own language. Buck and Matt cleaned, oiled, and reloaded their weapons. Afterward, while the others were talking softly, Matt seemed lost in his thoughts, standing by the window and watching the shadows lengthen and grow across the festering excuse for a town.

A knock at the door snapped Matt and Buck into action. Buck grabbed his Winchester and headed toward a back corner, where he would have a clear shot at the door. Long Ridge and Red Bird moved where they would be out of the way. Matt's Colt popped into his hand, and he headed for the door. Before he could open it, he heard, "Mr. Ramsey, 'tis Mary MacGregor."

"Is there trouble?" Matt called through the door, standing just to the side of it for safety's sake.

"Och, no, Mr. Ramsey," she answered brightly. "I've brought supper for all of ye."

Matt had a flash of worry, then discarded it. He yanked the door open. He grinned when he saw Mary MacGregor and a slim, teen-aged black girl standing there, each with a large tray in hand.

"Well, mon, get out of the way," Mary ordered in friendly tones, smiling.

"Yes'm." Matt hastily got out of the way, trying to slip the Colt into his holster as surreptitiously as possible.

Mary swept into the room, carrying the black girl in her breezy wake. There was little space in the room for so many people at the same time, so Mary and the servant girl set the trays down on the bed. With a cheery "Enjoy yoursel's," Mary was gone, the girl trailing afterward, almost lost in the gale that was Mary MacGregor.

The Ramseys and the two Cherokees stood for a few moments, glancing from one to the other and wondering exactly what had just passed through their small room. Then Matt laughed. "Damn," he said, still chuckling, "that was kind of like sittin' through one of them tornadoes we've ridden out before, wasn't it, Buck!"

"Worse, I think," said Buck with a laugh.

"Well, no matter," Matt said. "I'm hungry, and that food sure smells good."

They divvied up the food and poured coffee all around. "Hope you don't mind chicken, Chief," Matt said to Long Ridge as he handed the Cherokee a tin plate with pieces of fried chicken, biscuits, and boiled potatoes.

"When I'm this hungry, I could eat gophers, snakes, and spiders. Chicken don't faze me." He grinned, grabbed the plate, sat on the floor, and attacked the food.

Buck and Matt did the same, while Red Bird sat on the bed. She proved to be a little more feminine in her eating habits but no less voracious of appetite.

They finally leaned back, sated with food but still sipping coffee. Long Ridge lit up his old clay pipe and sat amid clouds of noxious blue smoke, puffing contentedly.

Some time later, Mary MacGregor knocked again. Once more she and her servant blew through the room, gathering up the dirty plates and cups and platters. Then they were gone again.

A few minutes later, Matt stood up and stretched. "I need me some air." He grinned at his brother.

Buck looked at him in alarm. "You think it's wise to go wanderin' around town, Matt? After all that happened this afternoon?"

"I ain't gonna go wanderin' around too much." He winked at Buck again.

The younger Ramsey was concerned. Matt had been acting so unlike himself since he was wounded by the Comanches that Buck worried his older brother was not right in the head. Still, he had seemed more like himself in the past few days. Matt was still staring at him, a lopsided grin on his handsome, broad face. Suddenly Buck had a flash of insight and recognition.

"Don't be gone all the night, Matt," he said seriously, nodding his understanding of what Matt was trying to get across. "There's a heap of unfriendly cusses out there."

"Not where I'm goin'," Matt muttered.

"And the MacGregors have been kind enough to keep the law off our backs. They don't need to be stayin' up the whole night to keep watch over us."

Matt sobered and nodded solemnly. "Good point, Buck. I won't be gone long." Then he grinned again. "But don't wait up for me."

"Bah!" Buck growled good-naturedly. "I'm of a mind to shoot you myself and save the sheriff the trouble."

"I was wrong, Buck," Matt said with a laugh, "when I said you'd make somebody a good wife one day. You'll make someone a good mother some day." He scurried out of the room as Buck snatched up a pillow and threw it at the closing door.

Feeling good, Matt headed downstairs and stopped at the counter. "I'm much obliged for you sendin' the sheriff packin', Mr. MacGregor. And," he added ruefully, "I reckon I'm sorry I said you wasn't a real Scotsman before."

"Well, laddie," MacGregor said in his breathless wheeze, "I'd say those words were needed. A man needs such a shakin' up of a time." He wiped sweat from his forehead. "And as for Sheriff Carstairs . . . that damn fool dunna know his arse from the side of yon barn. He'll nae give ye trouble—if ye're going out."

"I was considerin' it."

"Just watch yourself, Mr. Ramsey," MacGregor said seriously. "Carstairs might not give ye any trouble, but there's many another who'd do so."

"I'll keep it in mind, Mr. MacGregor." Matt took a step toward the door but then stopped and turned back. "But what about you?"

"What about me?"

"The good citizens of Calico gonna give you trouble for helpin' us out?"

"I canna answer that, laddie, except to tell ye that I don't much give a hoot what these folks try to do to me. They canna hurt me."

"Yes, they can, Angus," Matt said seriously. "There're some who'd as soon kill you and throw your bones to the wolves for helpin' Indians or black folk or any others who're different."

MacGregor shrugged.

"Or worse, they might come for Mary," Matt said quietly.

"Och, let them come for me, mon. I'm not afearin' of them," said Mary MacGregor, coming out of the back room. Her face was set and determined, but humor lurked just below the surface.

Matt grinned. He believed her. They would not be easy people to frighten—or harm. Still, Matt would hate to be the one responsible for them coming to any grief. At the same time, he knew he would never be able to change their minds about this.

"Well then," he said, "reckon I'll take my leave and go for a stroll."

"Enjoy yourself, Mr. Ramsey," Mary said. She turned and went into the back.

As Matt made to leave, MacGregor grabbed his arm. "Ye go down to the Muddy Bank Saloon," MacGregor whispered, pointing. "Turn right there and go down three doors on the left." He grinned, then glanced back over his shoulder to make sure his wife was not watching.

Matt grinned widely. "Thank you, Mr. MacGregor," he whispered back.

The fight that afternoon, when he had felt the sharp stab of pain in his chest, had let him know he was physically recovered. And the shootout afterward had showed him that his instincts, reflexes, and eye were slow after his convalescence but still better than most.

He had thought after the fight, when he was standing in his room staring out the window, that he was really back now, mentally and physically. But there was one more thing he figured he needed to make himself feel like a whole man again.

Two hours later, he returned to MacGregor's Hotel. Neither MacGregor was in the lobby, but he could hear Angus's stertorous breathing from the living quarters behind. He smiled and headed up to his room.

Long Ridge and Red Bird were asleep on the floor, but Buck was awake, sitting in the plump chair. Matt entered quietly and grinned as he tossed his hat across the room.

"Things go well?" Buck asked with a smile.

"I reckon," Matt commented noncommittally. "But you best get some sleep, boy." His attempt at sternness failed dismally.

"I'm comfortable here," Buck said. He squirmed his behind deeper into the chair. He was tired and would have no trouble falling asleep now that Matt was back safely. "Besides," he added, "an old man like you needs the comforts of a soft bed far more'n I do." He grinned and pulled his hat down over his eyes. "Night, brother."

Buck and Matt Ramsey strode brazenly down the street toward the livery. They received more hateful glances than they could count, but no one had the temerity to get in their way. They saddled four of their horses and then headed back toward the hotel, each riding his own animal and towing the others behind.

At the hotel, the MacGregors and the Cherokees greeted them. It took only minutes to load their supplies on the packhorse. Matt figured they had enough supplies—if Buck could augment their meat with hunting—to last them all the way to Sallisaw Creek.

The two Ramseys were even more wary than usual as they clopped out of Calico. It would be, Matt had warned the others just before leaving, a perfect time for an ambush.

But no one bothered them, and they set a slow, steady pace. Long Ridge looked quite handsome in his new clothes and tall top hat. He rode with straight back, and, despite the troubles in Calico, the old man seemed to have gained new vigor from the time there.

Red Bird was, as Matt had suspected she would be, beautiful in her bright calico dress, new moccasins, and bonnet covering her freshly brushed, shining black hair.

Matt rode sedately along, appreciating the time he had to think. He had been so full of pain, worry, and—yes, he could admit it now—fear for so long. It had made him unsure of himself. Until the events of yesterday afternoon and last night.

The traveling was as dull and plodding as it ever was. Along about midday, Buck pointed to the east. Matt looked over to see a small herd of buffalo. Matt nodded, and Buck loped toward the herd, pulling his Winchester as he did. He came up on the herd downwind, moving in to within fifty yards of the outer animals. The Winchester might be good against a man, but closeness was a necessity when using it on almost a ton of animal.

Buck dismounted and tied his horse to a bush. He moved a few yards closer and knelt down, aiming at a small cow. He fired, but it took two shots to put the animal down for good. The other buffaloes rumbled off to the southeast, followed by a cloud of dust.

"Move on over there, you two," Matt shouted at Long Ridge and Red Bird. Together they angled to where Buck was just a mounted speck in the distance. They were at the buffalo soon enough. "Help Buck," Matt said.

The two Cherokees dismounted. Matt returned Long Ridge's big Arkansas toothpick, Buck used his Bowie, and Red Bird used her small knife. They butchered only a small amount, since it would not keep more than a day or so.

Then they were on the way again.

Several hours later, Matt loped up alongside Buck. "I'm goin' down our back trail a bit to see if any of those damn fools back in Calico decided to follow us."

"Watch yourself, Matt."

"I will, Little Brother."

He was back in less than an hour. "As I thought, Buck, ain't a one of 'em got the nerve to follow."

Seeing no need to push themselves too hard, they began looking for a place to camp that night. They found a decent spot, better than some they had had, though worse than others. Camp was quickly and efficiently set up. It was as if they had been traveling together for weeks instead of barely two days.

Red Bird seemed to have grown less defiant, too, and she took over the cooking chores that night. Matt was surprised, and he expressed it.

"I just don't want to suffer through your brother's cookin' again," she answered simply, with a slight grin.

Buck, who was growing right fond of Red Bird, blushed with embarrassment. But after dinner he tried to stay up until after everyone had gone to sleep so he could have a little time alone with her. But he was too tired and finally gave it up, mumbling, "You best hit the blankets, too, Matt."

"I expect so," Matt answered and turned in.

Only Grace Red Bird was still awake, sitting near the fire, her knees up almost under her chin, her arms wrapped around her shins.

CHAPTER
★ 15 ★

Grace Red Bird never knew quite how close she came to dying.

Matt Ramsey acted before he was fully awake, one hand groping with fatal accuracy for the "intruder's" throat, the other wrenching out his Colt. He was thumbing back the hammer even as his eyes opened. He froze, trembling as his body craved some action to release the flood of adrenaline that was pumping, roaring in his veins.

"What in hell do you want here, girl?" he asked, his voice hissing quietly, revealing his anger.

Red Bird sat on her heels, her mouth a circle of fear and shock. She could not speak.

"Well, out with it," Matt ordered. He realized the Colt was still in his hand, and he jammed it away. He was frightfully angry but still full of wonder. Why had Red Bird woken him? he wondered. With a touch of worry, he tossed aside the covers, oblivious to the chill of the night air. He rolled up onto his knees, forgetting Red Bird was there for the moment. The worry grew. Had she woken him because the camp was in danger? Was something wrong with John Long Ridge? Or maybe Buck?

Everything seemed all right, and he sat back, beginning to relax a little as the pounding pulse of adrenaline subsided. He took a deep breath and asked in a whisper, "Are you gonna tell me what this is all about?"

"I . . . well, I thought . . . " She glanced around, hoping she had woken no one else with this little commotion, which to her had sounded like a train passing.

But Buck and Long Ridge slept peacefully. Red Bird gulped. She had never dreamed anything like this would happen. She had wanted to be nice to Matt. She had wanted to thank—no, she corrected herself, she had thought she *should* thank—Matt for all the help he had given to her and her great-grandfather. It didn't hurt that the big, dark-eyed Ramsey brother was rather handsome and, she decided, not an unlikely prospect for . . . many things.

But, mainly, she had wanted to ensure Matt's continued cooperation. He was, to her, a moody and difficult man, one full of boyish contradictions and oddness. One minute he was laughing and full of joy; the next he was a raging madman. It would not, she thought, be unusual for him to help them for a while and then drift off on his own, for whatever reason. Or no reason.

She wanted to have the cooperation and help of both Ramseys. She had decided some time just after the fight in Calico that she wanted to have both these hard-eyed, gun-wielding young men along. She figured it was the only way she and Long Ridge would be able to make it back to their village on Sallisaw Creek safely. There were many obstacles in the way.

She had offered herself to Buck and was still rather surprised that she had been turned down. She felt no sense of rejection from that; only a sense of wonder that a young man of Buck's age would do such a thing. She could not get over it. She knew Buck was interested in her, and she figured she could insure his help just by holding out the promise of the ultimate reward.

Matt, however, was another story. He was a harder case, older and wiser. Though she had known him only a matter of days, she knew he had faced hard times in his life and overcome all of them. Still, he was a man, and she had learned a lot about men in the past several months.

"Not here," she whispered. She stood up and reached out her right hand.

Matt took it warily and let Red Bird have the pretense that she was helping him up. She led him back through the hackberry and bramble bushes toward the river. It smelled on the riverbank, of stagnant pools and moist, dank soil. The humid, earthy odor was somehow comforting to Red Bird, and, to a lesser extent, Matt. As was the calming ripple of the water several feet away. The moon was bright, beaming down on them.

Red Bird turned to face him. She reached up, wrapped her hands around the back of Matt's head—having to stretch considerably to do so—and pulled his head down toward her. There was only token resistance as her mouth found his.

Red Bird could stand up on her toes no longer, and she finally broke away from him and smiled.

Matt was almost blinded by the emotions raging inside him. He was not sure whether it was love or just a man's natural desire when confronted in such a way by a beautiful, voluptuous, and willing woman. He had no doubts that she was willing. It must be only lust, he decided after a moment. There had been no time for love to bud, let alone bloom. And the face of Kate Silcox floated before his eyes, pale and golden. She was the only woman he had ever loved; the only one he probably ever would love.

There was a bit of relief. To think he might love this young Indian was ludicrous. But still . . .

"What was that for?" he croaked, his voice thick with the desire that boiled in his loins.

"I wanted to thank you for all you've done for Grandfather and me," Red Bird said glibly. She knew she was treading on thin ice. She was a little shocked by the hungry response Matt had given her, and she knew he was too big to be denied, should he decide he wanted to push her. But she did not think him that type of man. He would, she figured, let himself be tempted under the right circumstances, but she could not believe he would allow himself to lose control.

She shuddered, for another thought was even more disturbing to her. She was frightened and confused by her body's own response to Matt. It was a more powerful thing than she had ever felt before. With the Cross gang, she had felt nothing but disgust—and rage. But now, here, with Matt Ramsey, she wondered. It gave her thoughts that maybe this would develop and grow until . . .

Red Bird thrust those thoughts away. If she followed through with her plan, there would be no love developing between her and Matt. And if the plan did not work, she figured it would mean he was not interested in her. She decided she could not bear the rejection and that she should make sure that would not happen.

"That ain't necessary," Matt said gruffly. He felt a burning inside, and he fought it back. "And even if it was, you sure didn't have to wake me in the middle of the night to tell me."

"I didn't say I was gonna *tell* you thanks," Red Bird said, trying to keep the lingering doubts from gaining prominence in her brain.

"I just said I wanted to thank you." She looked at the ground in mock embarrassment. "There're other ways for a woman to thank a man she likes, you know."

"I reckon there are," Matt said slowly, his voice thickening as desire swelled up within him anew. "But that ain't necessary neither." He didn't want to say it straight out, but the main problem was that he was just not the type to take advantage of her.

Red Bird was taken aback. She had not foreseen this; she had not even considered the possibility. With Buck, as young and inexperienced as he still was, it was not so surprising. But to have this big, tough gunman turn her down was a shock.

"Not that I don't appreciate the offer," Matt said, his voice still harsh with desire and the lingering effects of having been woken so soon after shutting his eyes. "Another time, maybe . . ." He trailed off, not wanting to sound like a fool.

"You don't want me?" asked Red Bird, astounded that such a thing might be possible.

"I didn't say that," Matt retorted, regaining a little more equilibrium. "I mean you're a beautiful and—if I might be so bold—exciting woman, Miss Red Bird. But"—he shuffled his feet uncomfortably—"it ain't right. Not here; not now."

He did want her, and badly. But he was not the kind of man who could accept the favors of a woman who had gone through what Red Bird had of late.

Red Bird felt a wetness on her cheeks and realized with dismay that she was crying. The tears had come unbidden, but she fought the impulse to try to check them. Let them flow, she thought; they might do some good. She sniffled.

Matt looked distinctly uncomfortable. "Don't cry, Miss Red Bird," he said lamely. "It's all right. Things'll be fine." He was always at a loss when a woman cried. "I didn't mean no disrespect. . . ." He thought it odd that he would say such a thing. How could any woman—red or white—think he was being disrespectful when he was offering the utmost respect? It was puzzling.

"I know," Red Bird blubbered. Her sobbing petered out, until she was merely sniffing a lot and wiping away tears. "It's just that, after all I was put through by those ruffians, it's just so nice to find a real gentleman." She dabbed at her nose with the sleeve of her new dress, until Matt handed her his soiled bandanna. She used that to blow her nose.

"I didn't think gentlemen existed any more," she added, handing the cloth back to Matt. "After I was so ill-used, I thought that's all a man wanted from . . . from . . ."

She threatened to erupt into tears again, and Matt hoped silently but fervently that she would not. Matt was a tough man and had seen the world at its worst, but he had little resistance to, or comfort from, a beautiful woman's tears.

Red Bird managed to control herself with an effort. "I reckon I owe you even more thanks now," she said, smiling wanly.

"You don't owe me anything, Miss Red Bird."

"Well, at least let me *say* thank you."

"Yes'm."

"Thank you, Mr. Ramsey," Red Bird said, mustering up her dignity. "I am obliged to you and your brother and all you've done for me and Grandfather."

"You're welcome." Matt felt a little more comfortable now that Red Bird had calmed down. "Now, I reckon you ought to be in your bed, ma'am. We've got a heap of travelin' to go before we reach Sallisaw Creek, and you'll need your rest."

"Yes, sir." As he turned away, she said, "And Matt . . ."

He faced her again, and she stood on tiptoes to kiss his cheek. His stubble scratched her lips, but she didn't mind too much.

They walked back toward the camp side by side, but silently. Red Bird was confused. She wanted Matt Ramsey but was glad that he had turned her down. She liked him, but she didn't want to become entangled in anything. There would be too many problems. She was also disappointed that he had rebuffed her.

Red Bird was befuddled, too. She had not met a man with such inherent decency in a long time. She was not sure, at this point in her life, if she liked it, either. *What was it with these Ramsey men?* she wondered. *Were they all this decent and good? Or had she just met the only two of them that would act that way?*

She said a quiet good night and went to her blankets. Her great-grandfather next to her mumbled in his sleep and seemed ill at ease. Red Bird talked softly to him a few moments, certain the old man was not really awake. She lay down and pulled the blankets tight around her. There was a chill wind this night and a hint that winter was not far off.

Though she was exhausted, she could not sleep, as the thoughts, impressions, fears, and desires zoomed around inside her, often crashing into one and another. At times they would meld and offer a brief bit of seeming coherency. But then there would be another crash, another melding, and another reality. Irritated, she clamped her eyes shut and tried to will herself to sleep.

She must have managed, she realized, for she was suddenly conscious that it was just before the dawn. It was a time of stillness, with the night birds having fallen silent and the morning birds not quite roused enough to send out their songs. She savored the warmth of the blankets but knew she had to get up.

Red Bird was still sluggish and tired when she did so. She hurried to the bushes and then down to the riverside. She splashed water on her face, shivering at its coldness. Mist rose from the river, made eerie by the fading light of the moon.

Then she quickly gathered up a little more fuel, restoked the fire, and began preparing breakfast.

Matt Ramsey had trouble falling asleep, too. Grace Red Bird was an exciting and enticing young woman, and he almost groaned aloud at not having taken advantage of her when he had the chance. It wouldn't really be taking advantage of her, he told himself at least a thousand times. She was offering herself to him, willing and with knowledge. He just hoped none of the men he knew—especially Buck and Kyle—found out about it. He was afraid he would never live such a thing down.

He rolled onto his side, wincing as a stone jabbed him in the ribs. Perhaps, though, there would be other opportunities. His brother Kyle had found love with a half-breed—a half-Cherokee, half-black prostitute, no less. There was no reason the same couldn't happen between Matt Ramsey and a poor, hard-used Cherokee woman.

He drifted in and out of dull sleep, not really getting much rest. After what seemed like only minutes, he heard Red Bird rustling around the camp, and he knew the night was almost over. The smells of cooking food wafted to him, and he gave up trying to sleep. He got up and went down to the river to wash his face off in the cool water, hoping it would revive him.

Buck was up and about when Matt got back to the fire. "Mornin', Brother," Buck said cheerily.

Buck looked well-rested, something that annoyed Matt to no end this morning. Matt barely grunted a greeting at his brother. Buck, having seen Matt in the morning for most of his young life, grinned. "Decrepit old man," he mumbled.

CHAPTER
⋆16⋆

Buck Ramsey was feeling pretty good inside, at least for the most part. Grace Red Bird had been acting mighty friendly of late—since the day after they'd left Calico, as he remembered it. He didn't know why, but he was pleased with it. He had been worried after he'd turned down her advances toward him that he might have offended her, since she had turned a cold shoulder to him for a bit.

But, as he recalled, it was only the next day that they arrived in Calico and they had had the trouble. She just hadn't had time to get over the rebuff, he supposed. He had decided, too, that while he desired her considerably, he was glad that he had turned her down. He didn't know much about women yet, though he had some experience with them. He wondered if any man ever got to a point where he understood or knew all there was to know about women. But he somehow sensed that, in turning her down, he had done the right thing. It seemed inherent in him to treat women with respect. But there was more to it than that, he decided. It just *seemed* to be the right thing to do, instinctively.

He was troubled a little, however, in that Red Bird was also being nicer to Matt. Buck considered telling his brother what had happened between him and Red Bird and asking Matt to keep away form the squaw because Buck wanted to court her. But he could not bring himself to do that. He and his brothers—all of them—

might pull pranks on each other, might josh each other, might even rib each other about their sexual prowess. But discussing such things as these was another matter entirely. He finally just kept hoping that Matt would see his interest in Grace Red Bird and back off of his own accord.

More troubling to him was Matt himself. His older brother had been just about back to normal after they left Calico, and all through the day yesterday as they rode along. But today, he seemed quiet and withdrawn, holding a moodiness that was unnatural to him.

Near midday, Buck rode off on his own, looking for meat. As he was lying prone, sighting down the Winchester at a nervous, tentative black-tailed deer, the realization suddenly came to Buck. It startled him enough that he missed the shot. "Damn all!" he muttered, standing up. But he smiled, not from joy but from comprehension. To hell with the shot, he thought. He knew what was bothering Matt. Not that he could do much about it, but at least with the knowledge, he could be there if Matt should need his help.

They had been sitting at the breakfast fire that morning when John Long Ridge pronounced, "We turn northeast here. Away from the river."

"Why?" Buck had asked, curious.

"We gotta go northeast some time," the old Cherokee said. "Might as well be now." Then he grinned. "Besides, there's no decent crossin' where the Wichita meets the Red River. We'd only have to follow the Red, which goes southeast a bit for a while, as you oughta know, Texas boy." Long Ridge cocked an eyebrow at Buck, as if to question the young man's faculties. But he grinned, letting Buck know he wasn't really serious about it.

"Where do you figure to cross the Red?" Matt asked, his voice sounding a little off. Buck glanced at him, but Matt's face was serene.

"Near some place called Spanish Bend." He shrugged. "Don't know how it ever got such a goddamn foolish name."

Buck glanced over at Matt again. The older Ramsey sat with his face frozen in a grimace that was supposed to be taken for a carefree smile. Matt's eyes smoldered with a deep sadness and, Buck thought, maybe even a touch of fear. That's when he began to wonder—and worry some—about Matt.

As Buck climbed back up on his chestnut horse and rode off, following the deer, he shook his head. He felt a fool for not having understood this morning. He could have said something and ended his brother's worries. He sighed and pressed on, knowing the deer was gone. He hoped he could find another. As he rode, he brightened a little. Maybe there was something he could do. He pushed the horse a little faster, moving the problem to the back of his mind for the time being while he focused on trying to find some meat.

Matt plodded along, making a conscious effort to battle the demons that had arisen up anew inside him just this morning. He had been doing well. All day yesterday, Red Bird had seemed to be friendlier and more courteous. She had dropped her defiance and taken on many of the chores traditionally done by women around camp. She did the cooking, gathered firewood, and carted up water—the latter two with help, of course. And she did it without complaint.

Then came Long Ridge's pronouncement this morning on their travel plans. He felt an iciness clutching at his heart. He tried to keep a straight face but was not at all certain that he had succeeded. Now he rode on, the cold chill of—and he was mighty reluctant to admit it—fear his saddle companion.

He wondered how he would handle himself when they came to the Red River crossing. How would he act when he saw the two graves on the far side? he wondered. Would the bloodstains still be on the sandy, pebbled banks of the river? How would he react when he saw the boulder behind which he had hidden? And lay for God knows how long with a Comanche arrow in his chest? How would he feel, he wondered, when he came to the spot to which he had crawled, where he had come closer to dying than he ever had before?

He shuddered each time he was confronted with those questions. He had always considered himself as brave as any man. He had done some things during the war—and since—that might have been considered foolish. Things that had endangered his life. But he had, at those times, considered the risks worth it. He had been wounded a number of times and could handle the pain.

But there, on the banks of the Red River, after he, Marcus Book, and Jamie Cotter had faced that swirling horde of Comanche warriors, he had almost died. He had never before, even when wounded, even when suffering the indignities of the Yankee prisoner-of-war camp, considered the possibility of his dying. He had always been an optimist, thinking he would live on until a ripe old age, showing off his scars and old wounds to his great-grandchildren.

He could remember vividly now the first sharp pain as the arrow pierced his body and then the dull ache that radiated outward from where the sharp iron point had gone in. Things were hazy after that, as far as his recollection of events went. But the feelings and sensations were as lucid as could be.

One of the main things that troubled Matt was that he would act the fool—or act the coward—when he laid eyes on that cursed place again. He would never be able to lift up his head again under such humiliation. So he rode on, fear and worry swirling about his being like a cloak.

Buck came trotting back toward the group, a deer carcass flopping disjointedly across the horse in front of him. He stopped briefly and gave greetings to Long Ridge and a slightly longer, seemingly warmer greeting to Red Bird. Then he headed for Matt, who was, as usual, bringing up the rear. He no longer feared that the Cherokees would run off, but he was the most experienced in battle and had decided it best he ride back there to watch for any possible pursuit.

"You've had good luck, I see," Matt said, trying to keep an air of civil normalcy about him.

Buck nodded. He did not know how to broach the subject to his brother, but he finally just decided to come straight out with it. "I know what's been troublin' you, Matt," he said quietly.

Matt felt a twinge of self-disgust. So he hadn't been able to hide his feelings, he thought, sickened by that. "Oh?" he said, noncommittally.

"Come on, Matt," Buck said heatedly. "I ain't the smartest man the Good Lord's ever put down here on Earth. But I ain't all a fool, neither. It took me awhile to figure it out, since I ain't ever heard of that place Long Ridge mentioned, that Spanish Bend. But once it dawned on me where it was, I knew."

He paused and leaned over the side of his horse to spit. "Lord, Matt, how'n hell can you stand it back here, eatin' dust like this?" He grabbed his canteen, filled his mouth with water, and then spit out.

Matt had said nothing; nor was he amused.

"We don't have to go there, Matt," Buck said quietly, staring across at his brother.

Matt looked straight ahead, still silent.

"Don't you play that game with me, Matt Ramsey," Buck

hissed, his heat rising. "I ain't no little boy no more, to be put off cause you're scared to talk about something."

Matt looked at Buck then, and the younger Ramsey suddenly wished it hadn't happened. He did not like what he saw in those dark, brooding eyes. There was fear there, yes. But death, too. Buck shuddered, for he wasn't sure whether he had seen Matt's death in those eyes or his own. Either way, it was an uncomfortable feeling.

"You don't need to tell them others why we want to avoid that crossin', Matt," Buck said, gaining control of his anger and his own fear—of Matt and of what Matt was experiencing. "I'll just ride out again, tellin' 'em I want to check some things out. I'll come back in an hour or so and tell Long Ridge that I've seen a heap of Comanche sign about, all leadin' up that way. He'll most likely take it on himself to head us in a different direction. He don't, I'll just tell him that we're goin' off another way."

Matt looked at Buck, a flicker of hope on his weatherbeaten face. Then he grimaced and shook his head. "No," he croaked, his voice rusty from emotion and disuse. "I got to go, Buck."

"No, you don't," Buck argued. "You . . ." He jammed to a stop when he saw the determination in Matt's eyes and the hard set of his jaw. He nodded, understanding. Matt had to confront this fear, or he would never be right again. If he avoided this spot now, he would have to go through the rest of his life knowing he had been beaten by fear. Buck knew Matt could never live like that.

"All right," Buck said quietly. "But if you need to jawbone about it some, I'm here. You know that, don't you, Big Brother?"

"Yeah," Matt said diffidently. He could not tell Buck that he was part of the problem that had been vexing him since he was wounded. Matt had never been beholden to anyone for anything. But if Buck hadn't come along when he did, Matt knew he would have died. He owed his life to his little brother, a boy he had carried on his shoulders for fun rides until only a few years before.

Matt knew he also had to confront that problem. Matt knew that Buck did not expect anything extra for having saved Matt's life; he would have been insulted to know Matt felt obligated to him now. After all, Matt had saved Buck's life often enough and had always been there for the younger Ramsey when needed. But Matt was uncomfortable now that the boot was on the other foot. He figured, though, that if he went to the site and managed to work out his fears over it, then he would not feel so obligated to Buck.

Buck knew there was nothing more he could say to Matt. He doubted his older brother would ever come to him for any help. But he had made the offer—and meant it. He could do no more. He would not sit and worry about it. This was Matt's problem, and Matt would have to work it out as best he could. Buck clucked to his horse and trotted up to his position at the head of the procession.

The sky was just beginning to darken and the temperature starting to fall when Buck edged through some thick brush and a stand of cottonwoods. He felt his heart pounding, sounding like one of those big, thumping drums he saw in the fancy bands in bigger towns. He left the cover of the dense, silent foliage, feeling the need to urinate, as fear clutched at him. He came out to a spot where the land sloped slightly downward to a low, flat beach.

From his slightly elevated position, Buck looked down on the scene that had become so important in his life. It came back with a flash. He had just come to the spot from a different direction than last time, but, still, the scene was all too familiar. He looked down and could see Matt lying there, an arrow sticking out of his chest, another one from his thigh. He could feel the cold chill of fear he felt at thinking his brother was dead and the flood of relief that almost brought him to tears when he realized Matt was alive.

Buck did not stop, even as the thoughts tumbled around in his mind. He just kept going at the same slow pace, edging down onto the beach. *Christ*, he thought, *I hope Matt makes it through this all right*.

He rode toward the rock that had sheltered Matt during the Comanche attack, almost as if pulled toward it.

"We'll camp on the other side," Long Ridge said. It was more or less an order, though the old chief had tried to make the voice pleasant, so no one took offense.

He was shocked when Buck stopped Biscuit, twisted in his saddle, and glared at him. "We'll camp where the hell and when the hell I or Matt says so, damnit," he growled. He knew he had no right to take his worries and fears out on the Indian, but he did not seem to be able to help himself. He cursed himself silently for such behavior. In more even tones, he said, "Just head on over to the other side. Me and Matt'll catch up to you in a bit."

Red Bird rode up to him, her eyes wide. "You're not gonna leave us here, are you?" she asked, making her lower lip tremble some.

"No," Buck said flatly. "It's just that me and Matt . . ." He trailed off. He would not tell this woman what was going on. He could not. "We'll catch up directly. I promise," he said finally. "Don't you fret. Now, go on."

Matt was on the beach now and moving toward Buck, as Long Ridge and Red Bird rode toward the river. "Want me to stay, Matt?" Buck asked softly.

"No," Matt rasped, battling with all his considerable will and power the fear that clutched at his bowels and threatened to squeeze the life out of his throat.

After a moment's hesitation, Buck nodded. "I'll wait on the other side. I'd like to pay my respects to Marcus and Jamie," he said.

CHAPTER
⋆ 17 ⋆

Matt was sweating with fear—and from the phantom pains that flamed up in his chest—as he dismounted. He let the reins drop to the ground, knowing the midnight horse would not go anywhere. He walked tentatively toward the boulder that had sheltered him— was it only two and a half months ago?

A shudder of fear, like a large, dark cloud, passed over him. His insides were cold, feeling like death. He walked to the far side of the rock, where he had cowered—*No!* his mind screamed at him, *not cowered; took refuge like any sensible man would have.*

Behind the waist-high, ten-feet-around boulder, he turned to face the beach. He almost shook with the emotions that swept across him, controlling him. In his mind's eye he could see the battle. His breath rasped in and out as he recalled the fear he felt that day. He had fought in battles where the two armies numbered in the tens of thousands and had not been so afraid. But there was something about the dashing, wild Comanches that set even the strongest man's knees to quaking.

He could see the war paint on the greasy, half-naked warriors. He could hear the whine of bullets ricocheting; the heavy coughing of pistols and rifles; war whoops; horses; his own shouted curses and, dimly, those of the black wrangler, Marcus Book. He could feel the sweat running down his torso under his shirt; the comfortable recoil of the big Colt revolver; the satisfaction when he saw a warrior fall off his horse, killed by a bullet from the Colt.

And he flinched, almost groaning aloud, as he recalled in exquisitely painful detail the sharp agony of the arrow that punctured his chest, and moments afterward the second that hit his thigh, as well as the bullet that came. He sobbed deep in his throat, filled with despair. He was a coward! He would never be able to get this battle out of his mind.

Suddenly Matt felt himself leaving his feet, stumbling and falling backward, a moment after something exploded against his chin. His eyes snapped open as he hit the ground. Fear ripped into his guts, and he thought for a moment it might paralyze him. He scrabbled for his Colt, wondering what in the hell was going on; and battling to control the panic.

"Get your ass up and fight, you chicken-hearted sonofabitch," Buck snarled. The younger Ramsey was not quite sure what he was doing, but he knew he had to do something.

He had, indeed, crossed the river, following Long Ridge and Red Bird. But he stopped just after he got to the other bank. He sat there on Biscuit, watching as his brother dismounted and walked fearfully toward the rock. He could imagine that his brother was reliving the battle, and Buck grew afraid for Matt.

With growing terror for his brother, Buck reentered the swirling waters of the Red River and let Biscuit half-walk and half-swim across. He rode up, shocked that his brother was totally unaware he was there. He dismounted, leaving Biscuit next to Matt's horse, and walked forward, his boots squishing.

Buck was appalled by the look on Matt's face. The older Ramsey seemed to be in shock, his eyes closed. Soft moans escaped his lips. Buck heard Matt give out a choking sob. He was frightened, for he could see his brother deteriorating in front of him. The fright was fast replaced by a surge of rage. *How dare Matt act this way!* he thought. Then he thought, how dare God—or Satan, for that matter—steal his brother from him like this! This wasn't Matt standing here. Not really.

Without thinking about it, Buck stepped up and crashed a strong fist against Matt's jaw on the side of the chin. It was as if he were floating above them in the sky, looking down as he heard himself challenge Matt.

"Come on, Matt," Buck snapped. "Come on and get up." He flexed and unflexed his fist, shaking the hand from the pain in his knuckles. He had been surprised at the hardness of Matt's jawbone.

"What the hell is wrong with you, Buck!" Matt asked, lying there and rubbing his jaw, while keeping a wary eye on his brother.

"What's wrong with me!" Buck exploded. "Goddamn, Matt, you been actin' *loco* of late. You were standin' here near to cryin' like a baby cause you run into hard times at the hands of some damned Comanches. Shit, you ain't the first ever been set on by Indians, or outlaws, or just poor times the Lord's dishin' out."

He paused to suck in a breath and then started in again. "Well, you might be ready to give up, Matt Ramsey, but if you're set on doin' so, I ain't gonna let you off that easy. You want to give up, fine and dandy by me, Big Brother." The sneer in his voice was fully evident. "But I'm gonna knock the tar out of you first, so that when you do quit, you'll be able to say—"

Matt came off the ground and charged in one smooth motion. He slammed his shoulder into Buck's stomach. Buck hit the boulder and went over it backward, Matt following atop him, still clinging to his brother. Buck grunted and winced when he hit the ground, landing on a small, sharp stone.

"Quit?" Matt snarled. "Matt Ramsey quit? Like hell I will!" He began pummeling Buck.

"Goddamnit, Matt, leave off your thumpin' of me," Buck panted. "Goddamnit, leave off, before you get me fired up and angry!"

Matt stopped and stood up, moving back a step. "What's wrong?" he asked, smirking. His fears were gone, replaced by a searing rage. "You scared?"

"Hell no, I ain't scared of you," Buck said, also getting up. He tried to brush the mud clinging to his wet pants legs. "But you come at me again and I'm gonna knock the snot out of you."

"Me come against you?" Matt asked, bewildered. "Hell, you threw the first punch!"

"Reckon I did, didn't I?" Buck said with a grin.

Anger flashed darkly in Matt's eyes. "What in hell'd you go and do that for? That was . . ." He stopped, looking at Buck, who was torn between fear and hope. "What're you doin' back here anyway?" Matt asked.

"I was worried about you," Buck said simply. He rubbed the spot over his kidney where he had landed on the stone.

"I don't need nobody to worry over me, damnit. Especially no young snot like you." But Matt was not even convincing to himself when he said it.

"There's times everybody needs someone to look after 'em."

"I had enough of your lookin' after a couple months ago," Matt said bitterly.

"That what the trouble is? You feel like you owe me somethin'?"

Matt said nothing. Buck went to his horse and pulled two pieces of jerked beef from a saddlebag. He handed one to Matt and tore a chunk off the other. He chewed on it slowly.

"You've done enough lookin' after me, Matt," Buck said seriously. "It ain't no sin to need someone's help of a time. You start to needin' it all the time, then you got trouble. But goddamnit, Matt, we're family. It was never questioned that whoever was around would help whenever one of the Ramseys needed somethin'. There was no finger-pointin' that someone was slackin' off if he needed a hand. We just did what we did, helpin' each other all we could."

"This ain't the same, Buck," Matt said, sitting on the boulder and biting off a piece of jerky. He stared into space a bit, trying to find the words for what he was feeling. But he could not. How could he explain the stark terror that had enveloped him when the Comanches attacked and was repeated every time he relived the battle?

"Bullshit." Buck came and sat next to Matt on the boulder. He was comforted by the contact with Matt's hard arm. "Kyle went through hard times not long back, if you'll remember. A couple times. We helped him out. No questions asked."

"But I was afraid, Buck."

"We've all been afraid."

"But I was eaten up by it. It's like it took me over and was rulin' my life."

"There ain't no shame in bein' afraid, Matt. You've told me that yourself. You've told me how some of the boys in the war fouled their britches when the fightin' started. Did you think poorly of them?"

"No," Matt allowed, uncomfortable. "Not if they stood their ground. I got no use for a coward who runs off and—"

"You ain't run off from nothin', Matt," Buck said sensibly. "You stood your ground against the Comanches. Same with Mr. McFarrin's men back in Justice. Same with those idiots over in Calico. You've got nothin' to be ashamed of."

"But you had to tend to me for so long. I was useless."

"You weren't useless from fear. You were hurt. Bad hurt." Buck had a sudden thought. "You think somebody's gonna think poorly of you just cause you needed my tendin' for a spell? That it?"

Matt said nothing, but it was all the answer Buck needed. "Just call it payin' back for all the times you tended me when I was ailin' or hurt—or scared. You were always there when I needed you, Matt. You asked for nothin'; just offered. That's all I done with you." He rubbed his jaw, pleased to feel the stubble there: It meant he was fully grown now. "You were hurt and needed lookin' after for a spell. Now you're better"—he looked at Matt with a question in his eyes—"and you don't need lookin' after. Or so I'd think."

Matt was silent for some time, trying to sort out the jumble of thoughts that rattled around in his brain. Buck was right, of course, and he knew that. Still, it was a hard thing to face up to. But the worst was trying to face up to the knowledge that he had been deathly afraid of being afraid. And of dying.

He supposed that there was nothing wrong with such things. Fears like those were natural. He had just never confronted them before. He had come close to losing out to them a few minutes ago. But Buck had come along to save him from himself. And now he seemed to be able to look at those fears a little more objectively. He could be afraid; of that he had no doubts. He had been afraid during the war and afterward. It was what was done with those fears that had him worried of late. Cowards let those fears get the better of them. Strong, brave men—which is what Matt Ramsey had always considered himself—acknowledged those fears and then did what had to be done. He had done that, even if it took a little help this last time.

Matt wondered if that was perhaps a sign that he was no longer the man he was—or wanted to be. Suddenly he was sure it wasn't. He had almost given in to the fears and quit. But he had seen other brave men come to that point and get pulled back by a friendly hand. A hand—or a punch—that Buck had extended to him.

"I'll be all right, Buck," he said with quiet confidence.

Buck said nothing, but inside he was leaping for joy.

"But," Matt said, shaking his head in sadness, "I still miss Marcus and Jamie. They were good hands. Good people. I wished I could've done more for 'em. Or that I could bring them back."

"Well, you can't. You did what you could, Matt. Life's hard sometimes. And folks don't live forever. Those two gave as best they could, and they went proudly when their time came." Buck took another bite of jerky. "There's nothin' wrong with grievin', Matt. Jamie and Marcus were more than hands. They were friends.

And you'll miss 'em. So do I. That's only natural. But you can't bring 'em back, and worryin' over not bein' able to do so is only gonna make you *loco*."

"Where'd you get to be so goddamn smart?" Matt asked, looking at his brother and grinning wanly.

"I had a good teacher. A big, crotchety fellow name of Matthew Ramsey. A man filled with wisdom but one that's damn near useless in a brawl."

"Who?" Matt snapped. He gave Buck a friendly shove, pushing him off the boulder.

Buck landed on his seat with a thump. "Ouch, damn!" He stood up, rubbing his buttocks. "Well, if you're all that tough, next time we have a fight like that one back in Calico, help out a little, would you?" He grinned. Buck tossed away the last little bit of his jerky and went to his saddlebag again. He pulled out a pint bottle of whiskey and handed it to Matt. "As the *oldest* one here," he said, "you ought to have the first drink."

"Bah," Matt growled good-naturedly. He took the bottle, pulled the cork, and took a healthy swallow. Then he handed it back to Buck, who did the same.

They passed the bottle back and forth until it was empty, which didn't take all that long. It was twilight, and the sky to the east was a flat purplish gray. Insects were making their racket, and the evening birds were coming out to feast on the myriad bugs.

"We'd best get goin'," Buck said quietly, throwing the empty bottle away.

Matt stood up, looking around and waiting to see if the overwhelming terror encased him again. But he was over it now. He had the normal feelings of fear that an Indian attack inspired, but he would be able to handle them now. He said a silent prayer to the Almighty for being a Ramsey and for having a brother like James Buchanan Ramsey.

"You all right, Matt?" Buck asked, worried again.

Matt turned and smiled at him. "Fine, Little Brother. Just takin' a last look around. I ain't plannin' to come on back this way for a long, long time."

As they mounted their horses, Matt asked, "You mind if I stop and pay last respects to Marcus and Jamie? I never did get to do so, you know."

"Only if I can stand alongside you."

Matt nodded and pulled on his reins.

CHAPTER ★18★

John Long Ridge and Grace Red Bird looked askance at the two Ramseys when they rode up to where the Cherokees waited a little up the trail that wound northward from the river. They had watched the entire episode across the river and were wary suddenly of the two white men. Anyone who would act so strangely deserved scrutiny, Long Ridge mumbled to Red Bird.

"You know of a good place to camp, Chief?" Matt asked, ignoring the questions in both the old man's eyes as well as the girl's.

Long Ridge nodded solemnly, suddenly wary about his own and his great-granddaughter's status.

"Go on there, then, and start gettin' things set up."

"Why?" asked Red Bird. She had a sudden lurching of her stomach. Despite all her efforts, these two tough white men were going to back out of helping her and Long Ridge. Her mind was frantic as she tried to think up a plan to prevent that.

Matt took a deep breath to settle the sadness he felt. He half-turned in the saddle and pointed. "See them crosses over yonder?" he asked, turning back to face the others. When Red Bird nodded, he said, "Those're friends of ours. I never got to say good-bye to 'em before. Buck here buried 'em. We'd just like to stop off a bit and offer some words for 'em."

Red Bird felt a gush of relief, but she said nothing.

Long Ridge nodded in solemn agreement. "It's a good thing to do," he said, in somber tones. "A path cuts off northwest through the brush about half a mile north. Take that. Quarter of a mile on, there's a creek. Good water and good camp."

Matt nodded. Buck came up next to Long Ridge and transferred the deer carcass from his horse to the old man's. "Reckon it wouldn't hurt to get supper started while you're makin' camp."

"Reckon not," Long Ridge said with a grin.

"Thanks, Buck," Red Bird added. "But don't be long." She smiled at him, and his heart soared.

"Yes'm." He moved on, following Matt, who was walking his horse slowly toward the two rough pine crosses down by the riverside. He hoped nothing or no one had disturbed the graves. He and Luke Webb had not dug very deep graves, but they had covered them over pretty well with stones.

"You did well, Buck," Matt said after dismounting before the graves. He kept the reins to his horse in hand.

Buck flushed with pride. "I had help," he said with a shrug.

"From who?" Matt asked, a little surprised.

"Luke Webb."

"He that feller died in the soddy, killed by the Comanches?"

"The same."

"He was a good man, Buck."

"I know." Buck was sad now, too—something he had hoped to avoid. "Lots of folks gone dead on this trip."

Matt had been thinking the same thing. It had been ill-fated from the day the two Ramseys had left their shack on the Trinity—Buck with the McFarrin family and he with a band of horses he had planned to take to Fort Sill to sell. "That's a fact," he said glumly. "I'll be glad as hell we get back to our place."

"Me, too." Buck shook his head, looking over the graves. "I wished I'd had some plankin' or somethin' to've made them decent markers."

"They'll understand," Matt said softly. He thought about the two men lying here. Marcus Book, a black and an expert wrangler, had always been a man with a smile and a kind word for anyone, except those filled with hate. Jamie Cotter, young and full of energy, was nearly as good a wrangler as Book. It was pure hell for him to stand here alive, thinking it was his fault they were dead and buried.

Buck watched his brother. "It wasn't your doin', Matt," he said, almost in a whisper. "The Good Lord called to 'em, and they had to go. Whether here at the hands of the Comanches or sitting in front of the stove back at the shack."

"I suppose." Matt did not sound convinced.

But the more he thought about it, the more truth he could see in it. He could just hear Book's voice saying "De Good Lo'd bringeth forth, and de Good Lo'd taketh from y'all whenever he goddamn well pleases." It wasn't that Book had been an irreverent man; he just had his own way of looking at things, as well as of expressing them.

"You boys'll be missed by better folk than me," Matt mumbled. He could think of no more fitting epitaph to give them.

"I doubt that," Buck said.

Matt felt an increasing sadness. He seemed to have been plagued with bad luck most of his life. "I know the Almighty don't look on me with a hell of a lot of favor," Matt said. "I'm a sinful man, through and through. But I don't cotton to the Almighty takin' his displeasure at me out on other folks that ain't done nothin' wrong." He was changing from sadness to anger.

"It ain't right for you—nor anybody—to question the ways of the Lord, Matt," Buck said. None of the Ramsey boys had had much churchifying, as far as Mother Alice Ramsey thought. But she had made them go to church every Sunday—at least until they were old enough to rebel at such a notion. Buck had gotten a little less than the others, since he was barely eleven when Alice Ramsey died. But, for some reason, he had taken it to heart just a little more than some of his brothers.

"Bah." Matt often felt he could do whatever he wanted. He figured he was so far from redemption that nothing he could do would put him in less favor with the Lord than he was already.

"We'd best hurry some, Matt," Buck said apologetically. "It's near dark, and I got no hankerin' to miss that trail because of it."

Matt nodded. He said a silent farewell to his two friends. With a sigh, he took two steps, stuck his boot into the stirrup, and pulled himself up onto the animal. "Let's go, Buck," he said. He moved off slowly, looking back only once.

By the time he found the path off the main road, Matt had composed himself. He was back to normal. He would miss Marcus Book and Jamie Cotter, as he missed his parents, Sam and Alice; and his sister, Anna Louise; and his old friend, Knox Wapley, whom Matt had gone to help; and Kate Silcox. Missing Kate was the worst for him, and though it had been nearly seven years since she had died, the ache never quite left him. Yes, he would miss all of them. But life had to go on. He would keep a special place inside of him for each of those people, but that place would be closed enough so that it did not interfere with him. It would be opened only when he chose to open it.

"I'm glad that Red Bird decided she'd take over the cookin'," Matt said with a grin, as he smelled the smoke from Red Bird's fire and the venison cooking there. "Lord, I was gonna die if I had to eat your cookin' another couple of days."

"It kept you alive, didn't it?" Buck growled. He was no more fond of eating his own cooking than Matt was. He was not really happy at having to cook it, either, but since Matt was the oldest—and because he had not been himself—Buck had done it.

"I'll have to think on that a spell," said Matt with a laugh. It was good, he realized, to laugh again. It had been awhile.

The camp was simple but in order when they rode in. Matt felt an uplifting of his spirits when he saw Grace Red Bird. She was working by the fire, seeing to the roasting venison. Her eyes were teary from the smoke, and she had a streak of deer's blood across her forehead, from where she had absently wiped at stray hairs. But to Matt she still looked mighty good.

To Buck she looked just fine, too. But he was bothered by the way he saw Matt look at her. There was far more than just simple friendliness in that look. Matt looked at Red Bird the way Buck looked at the Cherokee girl.

The brothers dismounted, unsaddled their animals, rubbed them down, and stuck oat-filled feedbags over their muzzles.

They strolled back to the fire. Buck grabbed for a johnnycake, and Red Bird playfully smacked the offending hand away. "You can wait along with the others," she said, smiling.

He sat with his face aflame, because he knew Long Ridge and Matt were grinning at him.

Red Bird poured two cups of coffee, then stood up and carried them to the Ramseys. She handed a steaming mug to each, accompanying the act with a smile of promise.

Buck took the cup and stared at Red Bird a moment, then lowered his head, embarrassed. Matt took his and continued to stare, liking the appraisal he made of the young woman. She had changed considerably since the night she had offered herself to him. This was only the second night since that had happened, he admitted, but the transformation was welcome.

He retained a trace of suspicion, though. Red Bird was almost too good these days. She did not argue, she smiled most of the time, and she was ever helpful. Matt liked her that way, but he was not so sure she would not revert back to her old ways. He hoped this was the real Grace Red Bird and that the other had been a reaction to her treatment at the hands of Harlan Cross's men. He could always hope, anyway.

Supper was served, and they all ate quietly. Long Ridge had trouble since many of his teeth were missing. It irritated him quite often, but he was mostly used to it. It sometimes helped to ease his anger, however, when he paid more attention to others around him than to the trouble he was having in chewing his food.

"You were hurt back there some time, Matt Ramsey," Long Ridge said suddenly with utter certainty.

Matt looked at him in surprise. "How do you figure that?" he asked blandly, taking a bite of venison but keeping his eyes on those of the old Indian.

"It's in your face." He threw away a piece of meat he was having little success in chewing. "What happened?" he asked bluntly.

Matt shrugged. "Comanches." He clammed up, not wanting to say any more. But he knew he was expected to elaborate. He also knew that if he didn't, Buck would, and he'd make Matt's role in it far more heroic than it really was.

"Me and two others were taking a cavvy of horses up to Fort Sill to sell 'em. We were crossin' the Red when the Comanches hit. One of my men was on this side of the river, the other halfway across. I was on the south side." He shrugged again. "There was enough of 'em that we didn't stand much of a chance."

He fell silent and went back to his food. But he was not enjoying it any longer.

"And you lived?" Long Ridge asked. "Comanches ain't known for their goodwill toward others."

"I ain't sure what happened," Matt said sourly. "I was wounded bad and expected to die. Somethin' must've scared them off before they could finish me off. Next thing I knew, Buck and some others were there tendin' me."

Long Ridge started to say something else, but Matt snapped, "No more questions, Chief." For the first time, Matt used the term with some derogatory intent. He regretted it right away, but it was done now. "I just ain't of a mood to talk about it no more, Mr. Long Ridge," he added, more respectfully. "It ain't a topic from which I get much pleasure."

Long Ridge nodded, understanding.

Red Bird looked up at Matt, a sudden stirring inside her. She had liked Matt Ramsey a little before, but now that compassion was added, her feelings for him grew. He might be a good man to have, she thought, but she pushed that idea away. He was not the kind of man to fall in love with an Indian, she didn't figure.

While she was not really in the market for a white husband, she thought that if she had been, Buck might be a better choice. He was nearly as tough as his brother, almost as big and strong. Buck was certainly as fine a man as Matt. And he was a lot closer to Red Bird's age.

Not that Matt Ramsey was that old, she thought, giggling in her mind. He was, she guessed, in his late twenties. Still in his prime.

Red Bird sighed. Such thoughts were foolish, she knew. She wanted to keep both men interested in her enough so that they would continue to help her and Long Ridge. She could do that, but she was happy that it would not be an onerous chore. Both men were good-looking, decent men, and spending time with them was pleasurable.

She was confused, and she recognized that. But there was no need to rush in, trying to decipher the melting pot of emotions she had conjured up. There would be time, she guessed.

They turned in soon after they were finished eating. It had been a long and trying day for all of them. As they got into their blankets, Buck asked, "How long you think it'll take to get up to their village, Matt?"

"Don't know," Matt allowed. I never been up that way. If we don't have trouble travelin', a couple weeks, I guess."

"Ought to be easy goin', shouldn't it?" Buck asked. "We're out of Comanche country now, and that's a relief."

"I suppose. But there's other Indians through here. Kiowas and Cheyennes can cause a heap of troubles." He paused. "Plus we're in the Nations now. Didn't our little stay in Justice teach you anything about that?"

"Reckon so."

"I'm of the mind we ought to bypass any towns we see from here on out, Buck. Too dangerous. I've had my fill of such places after Justice and Calico."

"Amen to that."

CHAPTER ⋆19⋆

Buck Ramsey had never been an Indian tracker. He could track an animal as well as anyone, but when it came to following Indian sign, he was at a total loss.

Matt was better than Buck at such things, though not by much. His Indian fighting had consisted mainly of his fight with the Comanches only two and a half months before.

But both Ramseys were bothered by the signs they saw on the ground. They might be far from expert Indian trackers, but they had come across enough Indian sign in their time to be worried about what they had been seeing since two days after they had crossed the Red River.

After discussing it a bit between them, they approached John Long Ridge and asked what he thought.

"Kiowas," he said without hesitation.

"You sure?" Buck asked.

"Yep. Been studyin' the sign for a while. I was wonderin' when—or even if—you boys were gonna see it."

"We saw it," Matt growled.

"They close?" Buck asked, fear clenching at his bowels. They might be mostly out of Comanche territory, but the Kiowas had a reputation every bit as fierce as that of their long-riding allies, the Comanches, even as hard pressed as they were by the Army and the Texas Rangers. Buck had had his fill of fighting Indians.

"Close enough," replied Long Ridge.

Buck looked more frightened but determined. Matt looked grim.

"Which way do we go, Long Ridge?" Matt asked.

The old Cherokee grinned. "To catch 'em? Or avoid 'em?" He was not afraid. He was too old to be afraid. When he was a young man, he wanted to die gloriously. But now that he was old, he wanted to die in the peace of his bed in his village, lying beside his wife. Still, to die out here at the hands of the Kiowas would not be all that bad a thing, he thought.

Matt grinned back, but it was touched with flint. "I reckon we ought to avoid 'em, Long Ridge. It'd be unfair to them poor devils was they to have to face us after all the trouble the blue coats've given 'em."

"I reckon that's true enough," Long Ridge agreed. "Well," he added slowly, rubbing a hand across his worn, wrinkled face and prominent nose, "from the sign, they're headed mostly north and some west."

"Away from our direction," Buck said, relief evident in his voice.

"Yep." Long Ridge grinned again, almost enjoying this. "But Kiowas have been known to double back on their trail."

"Well, let's get movin'," Matt said. "If they are gonna double back, I don't want to be sittin' here waitin' for 'em."

They moved on, heading out into the treeless, lightly rolling flats. There was plenty of grass, most of it browned now after a summer of heat and grazing by the buffalo. But there was no cover they could use as a haven while fending off a Kiowa attack.

They moved with a sense of urgency, pushed onward by an imaginary army of Kiowa warriors. As they made camp that night near the only tree—a gnarled, scrawny juniper—they had seen all day, Matt pulled Buck aside. "We'd best keep watch tonight."

"You worried?"

"Wouldn't say worried, exactly. Just bein' cautious. You know such is my way, Buck."

"Want me to go through the night?"

"I'll spell you after a while." Matt was back to his old self, and he would not expect his brother to sit up all night on guard now, like he had done not so long before. But beyond that, he was hoping that, if he were on guard for a while, Grace Red Bird would pay him another visit. If she did, he half-hoped that she would repeat her former offer. He also half-hoped she would not make the offer. It would leave him in a terrible dilemma. He was still a young man, with a man's wants and needs. He was also a basically decent man, so he'd still feel odd about taking advantage of her.

He was irritated to some extent. He had come to realize in the past day or so that he was smitten with the young Cherokee girl. It wasn't love, but that might blossom, given half the chance. He was not sure he wanted that chance. It was ridiculous, he thought, to even consider the possibility. She was an Indian, he a white Texan. Any life they might have together would not be easy. She had been abused by men much more like him than he was easily willing to admit. It could never work. He was pushing thirty; she was sixteen years old—just about right for Buck, he figured.

That brought to mind another problem, one Matt did not want to ponder. He was wise to the ways of the world. He could see that Buck was far more smitten with the girl than he was himself. He knew, too, that because of such a thing, he should back off. But Matt would not. He had been through some hard times of late, a rough trail that had left him full of despair for a long time. He found that his pride would not let him give up this girl to Buck. He wanted to show his younger brother that he was still the head man of this faction of the Ramsey clan.

It was, he knew, foolish to think himself in competition with his brother for this girl. But he was, and that was all there was to it. There was nothing he could do to change it.

He tried to salve his conscience some by telling himself that he was actually helping Buck, anyway. It seemed obvious to him that Red Bird much preferred him to his younger brother. When Buck found out he was likely to be hurt badly, especially after just having been spurned by Miss Eula Mae McFarrin.

Matt and Buck cared for all the horses while Red Bird made dinner and Long Ridge rested his old bones. They ate and were soon asleep, except for Buck. The young Ramsey put on his slicker against the chill wind that blew down from the north. He patrolled on foot, circling the small camp slowly, with his Winchester in hand.

As he walked, he tried to keep his mind on thoughts of Kiowas coming to attack. But it was hard. He found it far more pleasant to think about Miss Grace Red Bird. He did not figure she could replace Miss Eula Mae McFarrin in his heart, but she would be an ample substitute—if only she gave him a chance to show her that he did care. She had been more than kind and friendly, but Buck was a little irritated by the fact that Red Bird seemed to be equally nice to Matt.

That galled him. How could she charm a man as old as Matt? he wondered. Did she think he would be flattered by her attentions and try to court her? Buck wondered. Or was it that she felt sorry for him because of all Matt had been through?

He sighed. He probably never would be able to fathom it. Still, the thoughts did make the cold, dark hours go a little faster.

Shortly after midnight, Matt relieved him. "You seen anything, Buck?" Matt asked, yawning. He rolled his shoulders, trying to drum up some internal heat.

"Not a damn thing." A somewhat disappointed Buck hurried off to his blankets.

Buck was tired in the morning, as was Matt. But they tried to be civil as they ate a hurried breakfast. They quickly saddled and loaded the horses and got on their way once again.

By midday or so, Matt was a bit relieved. He had seen little sign of Indians, and he began to feel they had bypassed any trouble from the Kiowas.

An hour later, Buck shouted. Matt looked up in alarm and saw that Buck was pointing to the northwest. "Shit," Matt muttered, when he saw about a dozen Indians sitting atop a ridge. He hoped the Indians had no companions below the crest. A dozen would be more than enough of a force to face out here in the open.

"Run!" Matt roared. He didn't know what good running would do, but maybe they could find someplace where they could make a stand. It seemed unlikely out here on the prairie, but it was better than sitting here and waiting to die.

They raced on, Buck far out in the lead, his eyes scanning frantically for any kind of shelter. Off to their left, Matt could see the Indians moving at a run down the ridge and out onto the plain. Buck noticed it, too, and swung to the right, hoping to make the Indians run their horses as far as possible before cutting off the small group of travelers.

Buck finally pulled up his horse hard, raising a cloud of dust. A worried glance revealed that the Kiowas were not that far off, and there was no place for him and his friends to hide. He had come to the lip of a buffalo wallow. It was the best they could hope for out here.

Matt had been wondering what, if anything, they could find for some kind of haven out here in this openness. He was not surprised, though, when he saw Buck pull up. He could see the Kiowas angling in. It was, he figured, time to make a stand. He was rather pleased that young Buck had shown so much sense. It was better, Matt knew, that they stop when they still had a little time, no matter how brief, so that they could have a few minutes to organize their defense.

Buck seemed to the others to get smaller as he headed into the old buffalo wallow. Within moments, Long Ridge pulled up in the slight hollow, followed by Red Bird and Matt. Their horses stood, blowing. Matt was out of the saddle before his mustang had stopped. "Keep watch, Buck!" he ordered.

The wallow was only four feet deep at its deepest, so Buck could easily see over it. But he climbed up to stand on the prairie, having a better view of the rapidly approaching Indians that way.

Matt grabbed the reins to Long Ridge's horse. Bending down, he grabbed the animal's right foreleg and tugged on it and the reins in the same direction. Under the pressure, the horse reluctantly curled up and fell on its side. It whinnied, wanting to rise, but Matt put his hand on it, keeping the animal down.

"Lay across his neck, Chief," Matt snapped. "It'll keep him down." He hurried over to do the same with Red Bird's horse and issued the same order to her.

He was perplexed about his horse, Buck's, and the packhorse. The latter was the only animal he could afford to lose, but he would be plumb sorry if his black mustang or Buck's Biscuit were to get killed. It would also leave somebody afoot—if they lived at all.

He decided quickly. Tugging his horse's reins, he worked the animal into position and got it lying down as close to Red Bird's horse as he could. "Keep both of 'em down," he commanded.

Biscuit was positioned next so that Long Ridge could have some control of Biscuit and his own horse. Matt speedily tied the packhorse's rope from its jaw to one of the forelegs, so the animal could move about freely but would be uncomfortable trying to move too fast.

"They're closin' in, Matt," Buck said calmly. The young Ramsey was afraid, and he would freely admit that to anyone who asked. But now that danger was imminent, he was calm. He knew what had to be done, and he was confident in his abilities.

"Keep your shirt on," Matt snapped, with a touch of jesting about it. "I'm on my way." He finished with the horses, grabbed his rifle, and headed for the "wall" of the wallow. Buck was already there, prone on the slight incline, his Winchester over the edge, waiting.

Matt crawled up beside his brother and whistled. "I don't like the looks of this," he said, understating their position measurably. He felt almost euphoric. For almost three months he had suffered both mentally and physically from the effects of being wounded at the hands of the Comanches. Now he was facing a horde of warriors as fierce as the Comanches; and he was at ease. He had worried for so long over nothing.

"And I suppose I do?" Buck snapped.

"I sometimes wonder about you."

Buck was about to retort, but Matt cut him off by saying, "I suggest you take down that one there in the big war bonnet first. He seems to be some big chief or something."

"My pleasure," Buck lied easily. He would get no thrill out of killing the warrior. It was just something that had to be done, and he would do it with as much ruthless efficiency as necessary. He moved a round into the chamber with the soft snick of a well-oiled lever and sighted.

He had had little experience with Indians. He had seen a few poor Caddoes and Wichitas and such when he was younger. But his first experience came only a couple months before, when the same band of Comanches that had attacked Matt, Marcus, and Jamie found him and his traveling companions. They had managed to find a half-collapsed soddy where they had fended off the screeching horde. Those Indians had been short and dark, lacking in color or spectacle, but they had been superb horsemen.

These Kiowas seemed to be almost as well versed in horsemanship as the Comanches. But they were far more colorful. It made them seem, to Buck, somehow more interesting. But he could not be concerned with that now. He fired once, and the bonneted warrior tumbled off his pony and bounced in the dirt.

Buck had no time to savor—even if that were a word he would have used to describe the feeling—his small victory, for the warriors were sweeping down on them with a thunder of hooves and a cloud of dust that clogged his nose and throat and made his eyes water.

Buck worked the lever of his Winchester and fired with smooth, practiced skill. He heard Matt firing beside him for a bit. Then Matt yelled, "I'll take the other side!"

Matt rolled over and up. He charged across the shallow wallow to the other lip, where he flopped down and began firing again.

The Kiowas had split up and gone to either side of the hollow; they collected at the other side, turned, and came back again. This time, they began circling.

Buck began to sweat.

CHAPTER
★ 20 ★

Buck felt almost serene in the face of the whirling madness. He fired until the hammer of the Winchester produced only clicks. A moment of calm descended, and he shoved a dozen shells into the tubular magazine as rapidly as he could, awaiting the next Kiowa assault.

"Matt!" he yelled, without looking back that way. "Matt? You all right?"

"Right as rain. You?"

"Just dandy. Long Ridge? Miss Red Bird?" he asked, a lump in his throat at the latter. "You folks well?"

"Yes," Long Ridge answered, for him and his great-granddaughter. "The packhorse took an arrow, though."

"Damn." Well, Buck thought, it wasn't all that bad.

"They're comin' again," Matt shouted, trying to wriggle his body another inch deeper into the dirt.

There had seemed to be no ceasing in the attack for some time, with Kiowa warriors circling, ever circling. They had ridden atop their horses at first, arrogant despite the initial killing of their war chief. But after three more had been shot by the accurate fire of the men trapped in the buffalo wallow, they began hiding by hanging off the sides of their horses, using the ponies as shields. But even then another warrior was shot, falling wounded onto the dirt.

His companions swirled in, screeching and firing off a fusillade of arrows and bullets, to pick the downed man up and race to safety with him. They took the time out of rifle range to regroup and decide if perhaps their medicine were failing them.

One warrior snarled and led the charge. The others glanced around at each other for a moment before following. The one headed straight for where Matt lay.

"Jesus!" Matt breathed as the Kiowa approached. "The bastard's gonna trample me!" He fired the rifle twice, missing the charging warrior, and then the rifle was empty. "Damnit!" He yanked out the Colt, but the Kiowa was less than ten feet from him now. He threw himself to the side. As he rolled over several times and then landed flat on his back, he saw a horrific, snarling face of black and red paint; and a Remington revolver was aiming at him.

Suddenly a round hole appeared in the warrior's forehead, and the expression on his face changed from one of arrogant assurance to a fleeting instant of shock, then slackness. The Kiowa tumbled off the horse as the pony raced through the wallow, barely missing John Long Ridge and the two horses the old Cherokee was trying to cow. The Kiowa bounced and then tumbled down into the hollow spot, coming to a stop right next to Matt, his expressionless face staring blankly up at him.

Matt glanced over and saw Buck grinning cockily. But that's all he had time for, as he turned and flopped back down to face the rushing onslaught of Kiowas.

Buck had rolled over onto his back, wanting to watch the Kiowa charge. He was amazed at the one who led it, a fierce-looking man with the sunlight rippling off his bronze skin. The warrior seemed as if he were going to ride right over Matt. Buck jumped up and watched with pounding heart as his brother fired and fired again, missing both times. As Matt rolled, Buck snapped the Winchester up to his shoulder and fired. There was the sense of a job well done when he knew he had stopped the warrior cold.

Matt glanced at him, and Buck smiled. It had an almost arrogant look to it, but Buck did not feel that way inside. He knelt back down and began firing the rifle again. He prayed that none of the Kiowa bullets would find him, exposed as he was at the moment.

The Kiowas split again, going around each end of the wallow. Both Ramseys followed, Buck to the northeast, around to the northwest, and Matt to the southern side. They fired calmly, tracking the Indians. Buck put two afoot and shot down one of them before he could be picked up.

He winced and almost dropped his rifle as a Kiowa bullet tore through his shirt, skimming his forearm from wrist to elbow. "You sonofabitch!" he bellowed. He fired off three quick shots, killing the warrior he thought was the one who'd wounded him.

The Kiowas headed off, and Buck figured they were going to regroup for another concerted charge. But they kept going, taking all their dead and wounded, except the one lying over by Matt. Silence descended on the small group. Well, not real silence, Buck thought. The horses still snickered and whinnied softly; and there was the far-off sound of horses' hooves; and, of course, there was the wind. But after the shrieking roar of the battle, it was silence to the two whites and two Cherokees in the stinking buffalo wallow.

"Think they'll be back?" Buck called, still watching in the direction the Kiowas had ridden.

"Don't know," Matt answered, also watching as the cloud of dust faded over the horizon.

"They ain't comin' back," Long Ridge said. The old Cherokee stood up, letting the two horses get up. He started to check Biscuit first.

"Why not?" Buck asked, heading toward the Indian.

Red Bird also rose, letting her horse and Matt's rise.

Long Ridge continued checking over the horse. "Bad medicine," he said simply, thinking that should explain it.

"What?" Buck asked.

"Bad medicine." Long Ridge straightened. "Damned Indians out here got some strange ways. Believe in all kinds of spirits and such that guide 'em in war and all. Their medicine goes bad, or someone breaks a taboo the war chief come up with in his vision, and they'll skedaddle."

"You reckon that's what happened?" Matt asked. He had heard of such a thing but was not sure if it were true. So many stories were told about the Indians—and by people known to be liars—that he never knew whether to believe them or not.

"Most likely. Hell, you killed the war chief first thing. Killed several others, and then this one, who decided he'd take over as war chief." He kicked the dead Kiowa in their midst. "You did all that and weren't hurt at all. When you shot this one, Buck, the others knew their medicine had gone sour. They circled once and headed off."

"Not entirely unhurt!" Red Bird said, pointing at Buck's bloody shirt. She started to go to him.

Matt looked up sharply. "You all right, Buck?" he asked, worriedly hurrying toward the younger Ramsey. He might feel in competition with his brother for the affection of Miss Grace Red Bird, but Buck was his brother, and he was concerned.

"I'm fine," Buck said, almost smugly. Actually, his arm burned like hellfire. But he was not about to let the others know he was in pain. It would be unseemly, he figured, after the wounds Matt had received not so long before.

"You still better let me tend to it," Red Bird said solicitously. "It ain't looked after, it'll fester up and rot on you."

Buck gulped at the thought, but he smiled bravely. "Do your worst, woman."

He sat down on the sloping grass and held out his arm. He did not see Matt's scowl as the older Ramsey went to help Long Ridge check over the animals. Red Bird cut through the bloody sleeve of Buck's shirt. She washed the wound out with water, then wrapped it in a bandage from a torn shirt.

"It don't look too bad," she announced, stepping back and wiping her hands on another piece of the cloth. "But I reckon it'd be wise to get some medicines for it. I know you boys didn't want to stop at no more towns, but I expect you'd best make an exception and try to find a doctor."

"Makes sense," Matt said, coming up. He was still feeling a little put out that Buck warranted extra care from Red Bird, but he could not stay angry at his brother for long. Not after his brother had saved his life—again. "Specially since we'll need another pack animal. And some supplies, unless you all have a hankerin' to eat flour with a touch of horse blood."

"I'll pass," Buck said brightly. He felt pretty good. Sure, the arm still hurt like all get-out. But he had been tended by Red Bird, who had focused all her attention on him. That was enough to keep any normal young man bright through a dose of pain.

Matt began to transfer supplies from the packhorse to the other horses, trying to distribute them evenly. Long Ridge held the rope on the packhorse, since the wounded animal was skittish and growing weak from loss of blood.

Buck walked over and looked at the animal. He counted three arrows and what he thought were two bullet holes. He reached up to help his brother.

"Sit down, Buck," Matt growled.

"I can help."

"You been hurt. Go and sit. I can handle this." There was no anger in the words; just command.

Buck thought to argue. It wasn't his way to shirk what chores needed doing. He had not been wounded many times before, and this was rather new to him. Perhaps he did deserve a short break. Besides, when Matt spoke in such a way, it was wise to listen. "Yessir," he muttered. He went off and sat down.

The adrenaline was wearing off, and the pain in his arm worsened because of it. He felt tired and wanted nothing more than to sleep. Even the company of Red Bird could not help him shed the dullness. "Damn," he muttered. With a supreme effort, he pushed himself up and went back to where Matt was working.

"I thought I told you to go sit your butt down, boy," Matt snapped.

"I can't do it, Matt," Buck said, trying to rouse himself from the doldrums. "I'll fall asleep, I sit there another minute."

"Well, I'm done, anyway." Matt wiped the sweat off his rugged face. Without much thought, he pulled his Colt and calmly shot the horse in the head. The animal fell, kicking. "Let's get goin'," he said. Just before mounting his mustang, Matt asked, "You well enough to take the point again, Buck?"

"I reckon." Buck felt like he had a blacksmith's anvil tied to each eyelid, pulling them down. But he nodded, trying to keep himself awake.

"You ain't, I can do it," Matt said, rubbing a hard paw along his stubbled jawline. "I can let Long Ridge take my place."

"I'll make out, Matt." Buck drew himself up straight, determined not to let this get the better of him.

Matt nodded, knowing quite well what his brother was going through.

They pulled out a minute later. As they were forming their line of march, Long Ridge pulled up alongside Matt. "There's a town by the name of Peaceful Junction up along the Washita."

"How far?"

"Ten, maybe twelve miles."

Matt looked up at the sky. It was lowering, and some snowflakes were falling. "Think we can make it before dark?"

"Probably." Long Ridge grinned. "Unless we run into some more Kiowas."

"Christ, don't even think such a thing." He paused, then said, "Peaceful Junction, eh? I don't suppose its name is accurate."

Long Ridge laughed. "It's a lot like that place Justice you told me about."

Matt nodded. "As I figured."

The wind blew colder as the day dragged toward a close and the snow fell a little harder. Still, it did not stick to the ground much, since the wind blew it along too fast. It did make for a cold, miserable ride, though.

An hour later, Matt spurred his mustang and trotted up to ride slowly alongside Long Ridge. "How far you think it is now, Chief?"

"Still six, seven miles, I'd say. Why?"

"You look half done in, Chief," Matt said, with an understanding grin. "But I'm more worried about Buck. He didn't get much sleep last night. Then with the fight, and gettin' wounded and all . . ." He glanced ahead at his brother.

Buck rode slackly, looking to Matt like a half-empty sack of flour. Matt wondered if Buck were even conscious. "I don't think he'll make it much farther."

"Seems unlikely." Long Ridge was exhausted, and he wanted to stop and rest his weary bones. He had, in the past hour, considered just giving up his spirit. A man his age should not have to live this way. But he was a stubborn old man, and those thoughts were fleeting. Still, a rest would be nice.

"There any place to camp nearby?"

"I come this way when I was looking for Red Bird, and I seem to recall there's a kind of hollow about a mile on. Good place. Wood, water from a creek that feeds the Washita." He grinned. "It's just off the road, too, so I don't expect it gets used too much."

"That important to you?" Matt asked, suspicious.

"Peaceful Junction's an outlaw town, Mr. Ramsey," Long Ridge said with a shake of his head. "Like so many others out here. That means a lot of such bastards roam around the countryside hereabouts. It wouldn't do to have somebody who knows Cross sittin' in our camp now, would it?"

"Reckon not," Matt allowed. "I'd not like any bunch of outlaws sharin' our camp, to be honest." He paused. "All right, your hollow is it."

Matt rode up to head Buck in the altered direction and tell him about the plan. He mentioned nothing about Peaceful Junction, though, for he knew that Buck, who was as hardheaded as his brother, would insist on pressing on until they reached the town.

Nor did Matt mention how ghastly Buck looked. The younger Ramsey was pale and weak. He rode with a grim look of absolute determination. *Christ, he's a Ramsey, all right*, Matt thought.

CHAPTER
★21★

Matt Ramsey was uneasy. He didn't like riding into a town like Peaceful Junction without someone to watch his back. It often led to trouble. But he was not about to drag John Long Ridge and Grace Red Bird into Peaceful Junction, either. That would certainly cause trouble with the kind of men who would be hanging around the town.

He didn't like leaving Buck to take the two Cherokees in an arc bypassing the town, either. There were too many dangerous men—red and white—on the trails around here. But that seemed the best solution to their problem.

"Don't stop for nobody, Buck," Matt warned, feeling like a fool. Buck was old enough and had been in enough dangerous situations to know what he should and shouldn't do.

"Don't you worry about us, Matt," Buck said, more than a little irritated that his brother would think him such an idiot that he would have to say something so obvious. "You just watch your butt there in Peaceful Junction. Those boys play rough."

Matt was irked, too, and about to retort, when he realized why he was angry in the first place: He found he did not like Buck riding out with Red Bird. The younger Ramsey had had too many opportunities, to Matt's thinking, to be alone with Red Bird or to have her hovering over him solicitously. That bothered Matt, and, in his own subtle way, he was trying to remind his brother that he was still mighty young.

Matt sighed. He was being foolish again. Letting this woman come between them was not good. Still, he didn't seem to be able to help himself. "I'll be careful," he promised.

He watched as Long Ridge led the way out of their camp, riding northeastward toward the Canadian River. He was followed by Red Bird, whose pitch-black hair glimmered in the early morning light, glistening with the dew. Buck brought up the rear.

Damn, if he ain't a man, Matt thought, still awed by the fact that little James Buchanan Ramsey was now nearly fully grown. *And one to give you a run for your money as far as the ladies are concerned, Matthew.*

Buck rode tall in the saddle, and Matt was convinced his brother had grown another inch or two and put on several pounds of muscle just this summer, since they had left their shack on the Trinity River.

Matt had some regrets, too, as he watched his brother fade into the thick mist. He had hoped—vowed, even—when their parents had died that he would not let Buck live the same life Matt had reluctantly carved for himself: a life filled with gunplay and bloodshed. Matt had never intended such a life for himself, either; it had just happened that way. He wanted better for the youngest—and favorite—of his brothers. But events had conspired against them both, and now Matt knew that Buck was too far down the path into a gunman's life to ever get out of it.

At least, Matt thought ruefully, Buck seemed well equipped to handle the hard life he had been dealt.

Shrugging off the gloomy thoughts, Matt pulled himself into his cold saddle, enjoying for a moment the sound of the well-used leather creaking under his weight. He breathed deeply—in, then out—the air steaming in the cold. There would be more snow before this day was out, he figured, as he turned the horse in the direction of Peaceful Junction.

The town was about what he expected: a motley collection of tents and crude wood buildings. Garbage was strewn about the streets, such as they were. The sun had risen, but it was feeble. Still, it brought enough warmth to melt the inch of snow that had fallen overnight and make a quagmire of the streets.

The people of Peaceful Junction—whether permanent residents or the hordes that passed through on their way to nowhere—were a rough and ill-kempt lot. By the time he'd passed four tent buildings, Matt had seen two men frozen to death where they had fallen asleep drunk; a fistfight; two dozen prostitutes, shivering in their scant costumes while trying to drum up business even at this hour; a shootout; and several drunken men howling and firing their pistols in the air.

Such things were why he disliked going into a place like Peaceful Junction. He thought more than once that he would purely hate to die because of a stray bullet fired by some drunken nobody in some hellhole of a town. He saw a small piece of plank painted with the name of Dr. Willard Carbo flapping in the wind. He headed that way.

He stopped and dismounted. There was a hitching post out front that looked like it wouldn't take more than a sneeze to knock it over. But since the mustang would stay anyway, Matt loosely draped the reins over the post. He was far more worried about someone stealing the mustang than he was about the horse running off.

Matt entered the doctor's tent. Several men lay on cots, under thick Army blankets. He figured the blankets were stolen, but that was not his concern. Most of the men looked in bad shape, probably suffering from a myriad of ills brought on by fists, boots, bullets, and drink.

"Can I help you?"

Matt looked at the short, wiry little man in the frock coat, colorful vest, top hat, and worn trousers. "You the doc?" he asked warily.

"At your service," Carbo said in a rough, raspy voice. He sounded constantly irritated or angry, or perhaps both. "Now, you want something?"

"Some medicine. For a gunshot wound."

"You ain't shot."

"Didn't say I was," Matt snapped, his own voice hardening. He had been in Peaceful Junction five minutes and already he felt a desire to burn the place to the ground. "My brother was shot in a run-in we had with the Kiowas. He ain't too bad, but we need some medicines that'll keep the wound from putrifyin' on him."

"Why didn't he come in here with you?" Carbo asked, no feeling of lightness about his words.

"He ain't of a mood," Matt spit, glaring at the physician.

"Well, I ain't so sure." The doctor pulled out a fat cigar and stuffed it into the bitter slit of his mouth. He scraped a match across his backside and brought it up to light the cigar.

He stopped, flame hovering, when Matt said, "You know,

Doc, these boys here are gonna suffer considerably without you to tend 'em."

Fear glinted in Carbo's eyes, but he managed to finish lighting the cigar. "Reckon I can help you, son. But I get paid in coin or gold. No greenbacks."

"Long's you ain't gonna try'n rob me, I got no problem with that."

The transaction was made quickly. Matt handed over some coins, and Carbo gave him some bottles and instructions. Matt nodded and walked outside. He stuck the bottles in one of his saddlebags.

Taking the reins of the mustang in hand, he walked slowly up the street. He saw a rough corral of posts and stopped at it. He silently looked over the horses within. Only two out of nearly a dozen looked any good.

"Mind if I look at a couple of them horses, mister?" he asked a man pitchforking hay out of a wagon.

"Help yourself." The man stopped, wiping sweat off his brow. "You aimin' to buy?"

"Might."

"Want to sell that black you're ridin'?"

"Nope."

"I'll give you a good price."

"You ain't got that much money."

"Reckon you're right," the man said with a grin.

Matt was not taken in by the man's friendly ways and easy smile, figuring the man would take him for every penny he could get, given half the chance. He climbed into the corral and checked over the two horses. One was in fair shape; the other was quite good. "How much for the sorrel?" he asked.

"Fifty."

"Hell, that sack of buzzard bait ain't worth five. I'll give you ten, though, out of the goodness of my heart."

"Shit, I got kids to feed, mister. I sell you that horse for ten bucks, I might's well just give him to you. Or shoot myself. My old woman finds out what I'd done, she'd shoot me anyway." He looked thoughtful, then said, "It'll break my old wife's heart, but I'll let it go for forty." He looked pained, as if he had just swallowed a mouthful of horseshoe nails.

"Twenty."

"Thirty-five."

"You can keep him, then," Matt said, turning away.

"Hey, now, wait a minute, mister." The man stabbed the pitchfork into the hay and jumped down off the wagon. "A man's got to eat, you know. Thirty bucks, and my kids'll have to eat beans for the next month or so."

"I'll think on it." Matt did not want to let on to the man that he only had twenty-eight dollars left to his name. "Mind if I leave my horse here?"

"Nah," the man said, disappointed.

"Nothin' better happen to him."

"He'll be all right.

Matt walked away, half-angry at being broke, half-amused at having left the liveryman flatfooted. He strolled to the first saloon he saw, a tent place with no name sign, only a painted piece of wood that read:

WHISKEY
BEER

He went in. The place was occupied by all sorts of ill-dressed and rough-looking characters. He went to the plank bar and ordered a shot of whiskey. He rolled the glass in his hands a bit, savoring the color of the liquid through the heavy glass. He was just raising it to his lips when someone slammed into him from behind. His whiskey slopped out of the glass, some falling to the ground, some spilling over the front of his slicker.

"Damn," Matt snapped, slapping his hands on the flat bar and shoving up and around. A half-drunk man dressed in filthy wool pants and short blanket coat was arguing with another equally disreputable fellow. Matt tapped the man on the shoulder but was ignored. With irritation, Matt pulled out his Colt and tapped the man on the shoulder with the barrel.

He was ignored again, as the man continued shouting imprecations at his companion. Matt grabbed the back of the man's coat in his left hand and yanked him backward, stepping out of the way so the man whipped by and slammed his back up against the bar, rattling it.

"I reckon you owe me a drink, pard," Matt said quietly, shoving the muzzle of the pistol under the man's nose.

"Go to hell."

"I'll find you there when I arrive. I—" Matt heard someone cocking a pistol behind him. He dropped into a kneel and spun around, his Colt coming up at the end of his extended arm just as he heard a pistol fire.

The man behind him gasped as a bullet ripped into his guts. The man he had been arguing with stood there with a smoking pistol. He was shaking, either from drink or fright, Matt didn't know. But he was trying to cock the pistol again. "Don't," Matt growled.

The man continued with his action, and Matt shot him once, neatly through the heart. Under other circumstances, Matt would have been satisfied with wounding the man. But not in a place like this. The man could have half a dozen friends.

Matt stood up slowly, warily trying to watch all the twenty-plus men in the saloon. He heard—and saw—a few pistols being unlimbered, and his mouth became dry. He was outnumbered considerably, though most of the men seemed disinclined to take part.

Suddenly someone was standing next to him, saying in a half-drunken slur, "I'm heah, Co'poral."

Matt looked over and nodded grimly at the bleary-eyed man that stood there, his pistol drawn.

"Anyone heah goes against Co'poral Ramsey, they'll have to contend with me," the man drawled. He looked a pitiable figure, but his eyes were determined.

"That's enough trouble for one mornin'!" the bartender roared. "Y'all put your pieces away and settle down."

Matt was surprised that everyone obeyed. He did, too, when he figured things were safe.

"A couple of you boys drag this dead riffraff outside," the bartender ordered.

"Thanks for your help, Bufe," Matt said, turning to the man next to him. "Can I buy you a drink?"

Buford Rice rubbed a grimy hand over his mouth, looking like he really needed a drink. "Yessir," he said quietly.

Matt ordered a bottle and said, "Come on, Bufe, let's set a spell. I ain't got much time, but I can spend a bit jawin' over old times with a friend."

"Yessir."

As they walked toward a battered table, Matt spotted a man in the corner. There was something familiar about him, but Matt could not place it. He shrugged and sat down. He set the two glasses on the table and poured them each a drink. He held his up in salute. "To old friends and men who fought together."

Rice grinned and tossed the shot back straight off. He looked longingly at the bottle.

"Help yourself," Matt said with a smile. It hurt him, though, to see his old comrade in arms in such shape. Buford Rice had been a good soldier, as brave and true as any Matt had ever met. But now he was reduced to grubbing drinks in a place like this.

"What in hell's happened to you, Bufe?" Matt asked, concerned.

Rice shrugged. "Powerful hard times come on me after the war, Matt. Lucinda passed on in childbirth. I lost the young 'uns to fever soon after." He gulped the drink. "Things just fell apart after that."

Matt nodded sadly. He had seen it happen before. Rice had probably fallen in with the wrong people after his personal troubles, and now he was so far down he could never be helped back up again. It saddened—and sickened—Matt.

CHAPTER
★ 22 ★

"Damn!" Matt snapped.

Buck, riding next to him as their horses swam across the cold South Canadian River, looked at his brother in alarm. "What's wrong, Matt?" he asked, his eyes wide and worried.

But Matt was so angry at himself that all he could do was mutter, "Damn, damn, damn!"

"Christ, Matt, tell me what's gone wrong!" Buck demanded.

"On the other side," Matt growled, letting his anger sift and simmer deep down in his belly. His anger had started back in Peaceful Junction. He was unhappy about being forced into killing someone, and he was irked that he was nearly out of cash. Mainly, though, he was angry at Buford Rice's condition and at not being able to help his former army companion.

He had spent a little time talking with Rice, rehashing old times, and watching with sadness as Rice poured shot after shot of whiskey down his gullet. But finally Matt knew he had to leave. "I don't suppose," he said carefully, "that either of those two dead boys has horses?"

"Naw, sir. But they had mules."

"Reckon that'd do. I just need a pack animal."

"Them boys sho' as hell won't need 'em no mo'."

"Where would I find 'em?"

"The livery."

"Well, Bufe, I'd best be on my way."

"There's still half a bottle left," Rice said, half in expectation, half in sadness.

"Keep it."

Rice's eyes gleamed. "Tell you what, Matt: I'll walk down to the livery with y'all. Make sure Krechner don't give y'all a hard time over them mules."

Matt nodded and stood up. He took note again of the man at the corner table. The man wore an odd hat for such a man in such a place, and he seemed to be watching Matt. The man seemed somehow familiar, but Matt still could not place him. Matt shrugged and walked out, followed by Rice, who carefully carried his bottle of whiskey.

Krechner was of a mind to give Matt a hard time. He was going to lose a sale on the horse Matt had looked at earlier, and now Matt was going to take two mules the man would have been able to sell later. But Rice's soothing explanation and Matt's steely glare calmed him.

Matt gave Krechner two dollars for caring for the mustang and three dollars for having taken care of the dead men's mules for the past several days. That helped mollify the liveryman. After Krechner went back to his work, Matt handed Rice fifteen dollars.

"I cain't take this, Co'poral," Rice said earnestly, though his eyes glittered with desire.

"Call it a payback for helpin' an old friend." He paused. "It's yours to do with what you want, Bufe, but I'd recommend you clean yourself up and get the hell back to Texas. Maybe you can find decent work down there."

"I'll think on it, Matt," Rice said, but Matt knew the man was lying. He would go and spend that fifteen dollars on whiskey and maybe a woman without so much as a second thought.

Matt nodded and mounted up. He rode slowly out of town, but as soon as he was out of sight of Peaceful Junction, he kicked the mustang into a trot. The two mules, tugged behind the horse by a rope, did not take kindly to the pace, but they fell into the rhythm after a little.

He had caught up to his brother and the two Cherokees before midday, with more light snowflakes falling. As he fell in beside his brother, Matt said, "I met Bufe Rice back there in Peaceful Junction. You remember Bufe, don't you?"

"Sure. I used to see him and his brother Otis of a time in church. How's he doin'?"

"He's a damned drunk, useless to himself and everyone else."

Buck glanced at Matt and felt his brother's hurt. He nodded and said nothing.

"He did stand up with me, though," Matt said very quietly. He explained about his venture into Peaceful Junction. When he was done, they rode in silence for a while, before Matt asked, "You want I should dose you with some medicine?"

"It can hold."

Two hours later, they edged into the cold South Canadian River. There were a few scary moments on the way across the wide river, but they all made it. As soon as he was on firm ground, Matt shouted, "Buck, Miss Red Bird, gather up some wood. We'll stop here for a spell."

Long Ridge sat down and wrapped himself in a blanket; he was shivering. Red Bird and Buck hurriedly began grabbing sticks and branches, as Matt began tending to the horses. After dropping her initial load of fuel, Red Bird set about making a fire, while Buck continued picking up wood.

The fire was soon roaring merrily, making a welcome counterpoint to the sifting snowflakes. Matt finished with the animals and came to stand by the fire, rubbing his hands. "I'd suggest," he said, "that we all get out of these wet duds so we don't catch our death."

Buck had already figured on doing just that. Though it was warm by the fire, he knew it should be done soon. He hurried over and grabbed his extra pair of pants and only extra pair of socks. There was nothing he could do about the boots. He hurried behind a bush and changed rapidly, pushed on by not wanting to get caught half-naked by Red Bird—and because it was cold.

Then it was Matt's turn. After him, the two Ramseys carried Long Ridge behind a bush and helped the shivering old man change. Then they helped him back to the fire. Red Bird was cooking and tried to put off changing, but Matt glared at her until she acquiesced.

As they finally began to eat, crowded around the fire, Buck said, "Spill it, Matt."

Matt looked sour and glanced from Red Bird to Long Ridge.

"Spill what?" Red Bird asked, trying to sound bright.

Matt kept mum.

"These two've been with us long enough that they can be trusted, Matt. If you have news that affects one—or all—of us, let it out. They got a right to know."

"Yeah," Matt said with a breath. He took a bite of corncake and chewed it a moment. "I saw Garrick O'Fallon in the saloon in Peaceful Junction. I thought he looked familiar, but I didn't realize who he was till we were crossin' the river."

"Who's he?" Red Bird asked.

"You remember we told you about the stage holdup?" When Red Bird nodded, Matt said, "O'Fallon was the one who got away."

"So?"

"The stage driver told us O'Fallon usually rides with Harlan Cross."

"What's that got to do with us?" Buck asked. "He never saw who it was who shot down his pards."

"That stage driver struck me as a man who flaps his gums an awful lot. I expect he blabbed our names all over Jacksboro once he got there."

"I still don't see the point. Even if word got out that we were involved somehow, how's he gonna know who we are? Or where we are?"

Matt looked rueful. "As me and Bufe were jawin' over old times, he asked what I was doin'. So I told him. It wasn't till later that I noticed O'Fallon. I expect he was listenin' the whole while."

"You think he'll bring Cross after us?"

"He seems the sort."

"We're in a pickle, ain't we, Matt?" Buck asked. He didn't sound worried; he was just stating a fact.

"Could be."

"Why would we be in trouble?" Red Bird asked, her eyes zipping from Matt's to Buck's and back.

"I expect he'll have a good-sized company of boys to bring along with him. You should know that. And ain't but me and Buck in fightin' shape."

"So? He'll never find us."

"Like hell. There might not be many towns up here, but there's enough. And travelers. Word'll get around. He'll find us if he puts his mind to it."

"How's anyone gonna know it's us?"

"How many white gunmen are ridin' around this country with a beautiful Cherokee girl and an old Cherokee chief?" Matt asked sourly.

"Oh."

"Yes, oh."

"But," said Red Bird slowly, "if we ride hard, we should be able to get back to our village before he could find us."

Matt was about to answer, but Long Ridge spoke first: "And what good do you think that'll do, Granddaughter?"

"Well, we could . . ."

"Harlan Cross stole you from our village with no resistance from our people. They will do nothing to help us now, either."

"Then what do we do?" Red Bird asked, dejected. Her meal was forgotten.

Matt sat quietly for a while, eating. He did not much taste the food, but he knew he needed it for strength and warmth. Finally he set his plate down and wiped his hands on his pants. "I reckon we run as hard as we can, till we find a place to make a stand."

The others were silent, not thinking it the best plan they had ever heard. Indeed, it sounded downright futile to them. But none could come up with anything better.

"We'd best be movin' soon," Matt said finally. "Miss Red Bird, please see to Buck's arm. There are medicines and clean bandaging material in my saddlebags. Chief, I know this is beneath you, but do you expect you could clean up these meal things?"

The old chief nodded gravely. Such work was, indeed, beneath him. But times were hard, and everyone had to do his share. Besides, he had suffered far worse humiliations in his life. Cleaning up a few dishes and such would be no problem.

Matt nodded. "I'll saddle the horses and pack the mules."

They were done soon and on their way. Matt kept riding along their back trail, watching for any pursuit. But none came that day. Nor the next, nor the next. Some time late in the following morning, they crossed the North Canadian.

It had rained the day before, and the river was running swift, sure and cold. One of the two mules, weaker than the other, struggled against the rope, tugged by the swift current. It brayed and honked. Red Bird fought with all her young strength to control the mules, as well as her mount, which was becoming increasingly nervous by all the commotion behind.

"Come on, boy," Matt cooed to the black mustang. The animal responded well, moving up strongly. Matt pulled his big knife as he came up alongside the hard-pressed mule. He reached over and, with one swift move, sliced the rope. The braying mule, too feeble to fight, was swept away by the freezing current, its head bobbing barely above the water. Its cries faded within a short distance, dwarfed by the heavily rippling water.

Matt moved up, urging his horse on. He came alongside the other mule, the one with all their supplies. He grabbed the rope and, riding just about abreast of Red Bird, helped tow the animal toward the northern bank. He glanced ahead and saw Buck, wind whipping his sandy hair as his hat hung by a thong down his back, struggling to get Long Ridge up the bank.

They stopped on the bank and built a fire to dry and warm themselves, like they had when they crossed the South Canadian. And they took some time to rest. They had been pushing hard, and Long Ridge looked pretty well done in.

"Maybe we ought to stay the night here, Matt," Buck said quietly as they stood on the riverbank, watching the rushing waters.

"It'd be risky."

"Maybe." Buck shrugged. "But we ain't seen no sign of Cross. And we keep on pushin' like we've been doin', and old Long Ridge ain't gonna make it."

"I know," Matt said wearily. He looked at Buck and realized he was staring almost directly into his younger brother's eyes. "Seems you've growed considerable of late, Buck," he said with a slight smile.

"Suppose I have." Buck was torn. He loved his brother, but there still remained the matter of Grace Red Bird between them. Buck thought it would have been better had Eula Mae McFarrin accepted his plea to come courting. Then none of this would've happened. He realized that his brother also knew there was a rift between them, and he was shocked. *Could Matt really like Red Bird?* he wondered. He shook it off. This was not the time nor the place to be worrying about his growing affection for Red Bird, nor the possibility that his brother might also be sweet on the Cherokee girl. They had more important things to worry about.

Matt looked out at the river for a few more minutes. Then he nodded. "Reckon it'll be safe enough."

They stayed the night there, supping on the finest cuts of a fresh buffalo cow Buck had brought down early in the afternoon. After their feast, Matt said, "You know, Long Ridge, I ain't so sure Red Bird didn't have a good idea."

"What's that?" the old chief asked. He was tired, and it made him less interested than he knew he should be.

"Head for your village."

"I told you what was wrong with that," he said grumpily.

"I know. But ain't there forts up that way?"

"A couple. But those bastard blue bellies ain't gonna help a couple Cherokees in trouble."

"Maybe not. But they might help a couple of good Texans."

"Could be worth a shot," Long Ridge admitted grudgingly. "If we can make it that far."

No one said anything. Matt knew the others might think him crazy, but he was certain Harlan Cross and his band of owlhoots would be on their trail sooner or later.

CHAPTER
★ 23 ★

Matt Ramsey sat on a ridge, looking back the way he and the others had come. The ridge was covered with a dusting of snow, but the day was clear and bright—and cold. Matt could see riders a ways off in the distance, coming at a steady pace.

He pulled out an old collapsing telescope, opened it, and peered through it at the riders. He had never seen Harlan Cross, so he had no idea what the man looked like. But he did know Garrick O'Fallon, and it was easy to pick out that outlaw's gray derby with the gold eagle pin gleaming in the sunlight.

He felt a grim satisfaction in knowing he had been right all along about Cross pursuing them. They had ridden hard for several days, always watching their back trail. They had skirted three towns, not wanting to be seen, and had once hidden in some brush as two rough-looking men passed by. The others had begun to doubt that Matt knew what he was talking about, but now he felt vindicated.

Not that he was happy about the situation. Cross had thirteen riders with him, Matt counted. Not a pleasant thought, him and Buck having to face down fourteen hardened outlaws. Still, he had been in tighter spots before.

He stuffed the telescope back into itself and dropped it into one of his saddlebags. He watched the distant riders a moment more before pulling the mustang around. "Time for business, boy," he muttered, slapping the horse's flank with the long loose end of the reins.

The others were about a mile ahead as he came to the open flat at the foot of the ridge, and it was but a few minutes before he caught up to Buck, Long Ridge, and Red Bird. He rode straight up to his brother and stopped him. Long Ridge and Red Bird came up.

"Cross's comin', folks," he said, without preliminary.

"I don't suppose he's alone," Buck said with a tight smile.

"Not hardly. I counted fourteen of 'em."

"Damn!" Buck breathed for all of them. "How far?"

"Couple miles, at most."

"You got any bright ideas, Matt?" Buck asked roughly. He was irritated that his brother had been right. He was also not happy with this turn of events. He wanted only to get to Long Ridge's village up on Sallisaw Creek and then decide how to court Red Bird. And how to deal with his brother as far as Red Bird was concerned. It had been worrying him more and more the closer they got to the Cherokees' home, and that did not help his mood. Neither did this latest bit of news.

"Nope," Matt said, uncomfortable. He wished his brother Kyle were with them. That would go a far piece in cutting down the odds. But they would have to do with what they had. He looked around. There was nothing to be seen.

The land was deceptive in that it was not perfectly flat but rather bunched and rolled. But those dips and gullies would offer no protection, no place to mount a defense against more than a dozen armed and cold-hearted killers.

"They comin' hard?" Long Ridge asked. The old Cherokee looked pasty from cold and exhaustion.

"They ain't out for a Sunday stroll," Matt snapped, growing more angry with their situation. He wondered how he had ever been roped into this venture. Then he looked at Red Bird, and he knew.

Red Bird looked scared and cold and tired. But she was still beautiful to Matt. Matt might not want to marry her, but he would sure as all get-out like to spend some time with her—alone. A flicker of anger at his brother sparked up.

"But they ain't runnin' hard at us, are they?" Long Ridge asked for the second time.

Matt shook his head to break himself of the thoughts. "No. But they'll catch up soon enough."

"But we've got a little time." Long Ridge fought to dispel the lethargy that afflicted him. Getting old was hell, he thought, and right now he wished he had died a young man, back in the old days before the Long Walk. But such hoping was futile.

"I reckon." Matt took another look around. "You got somethin' in mind, Chief?"

Long Ridge nodded slowly, the weight of years, fear, and infirmity trying to crush him. "If we push—hard—we might make the Arkansas. There's a lot of places there with thickets and trees. We could make a stand there."

"Reckon we got no choice, though it doesn't sound too good," Matt allowed. But he felt a glimmer of hope.

Long Ridge threw back his thin shoulders and puffed out his chest as far as it would go. "And when we are there," he said with grave dignity, "I, John Long Ridge, will ride on and bring help from Fort Chickamauga."

"No!" Red Bird gasped.

"Yes, Granddaughter," said Long Ridge solemnly.

"No. I will go."

"You are young," Long Ridge said, his voice rebuking her for questioning the decision of a warrior—and a chief. "You can help Matt and Buck with the fightin'."

Red Bird started to argue, but she stopped without saying anything, her defiance wilting under the harsh glares from the two Ramseys.

"We'd best ride, then," Matt said with sudden urgency. "And hard."

Buck slapped Biscuit and took off. The others raced off after him. They galloped on sure and steady, never slackening, mile after mile. Some time after noon, Buck topped one of the interminable little rises and spotted the upper branches of trees in the distance. A half-mile, he estimated.

Matt saw them, too, and he stopped, waiting on the little hump of a hill and watching their back trail. Minutes later he saw the horsemen coming, rolling over a ridge a little more than a mile away. Matt turned his mustang and raced on after the others.

Buck came up out of a gully and slowed his horse as he neared the thickets that lined the banks of the Arkansas River to a depth of anywhere from five feet to thirty yards. Tall cottonwoods, their bare branches dancing in the wind, rose out of the bushes. Buck saw the thin thread of a path winding into the thicket, and he moved that way.

The constant wind was calmed here in the cover of the greenery, making it seem a little warmer. A few yards off the path Buck saw an opening leading to a small, roughly circular clearing about twenty feet around. Buck pulled in and stopped in the clearing. Grabbing his Winchester, he made a circuit of the clearing, peering through the foliage. He even shoved his way through some of the brush, testing its strength and protective powers. He nodded. "This is as good as we're gonna find, I reckon," he said, without equivocation.

The brush covering the area from which the attack would have to come was covered with thorns and brambles. It was thick and interlaced with smaller trees; cottonwoods would offer protection. The brush on the sides was not as thick but substantial, and any enemy would have a hard time working his way through the area unseen or unheard. Behind them they would have the safety of the wide Arkansas and the brush that crowded the bank.

Matt pushed through and into the clearing, dismounting. "They're comin'," he said. "A mile or so back."

Buck nodded. "Gives us a little time to get set."

"Well," Long Ridge said seriously from atop his horse. "I'd best be on my way."

Matt grabbed his reins. "You ain't goin' nowhere, Chief."

"But we decided," Long Ridge protested. He had seen a last chance to gain glory and honors that he had not seen in forty years. Now it was being snatched away from him again.

"It's too dangerous right now," Matt said. He knew what the old man was feeling, but he did not want to argue about it.

"It's . . ."

"Save your breath, Chief. It's too dangerous. Those bastards'll be here before you could get halfway across the river. You'd be easy pickin's sittin' out there. Maybe after dark." He did not add the thought he had that they might not be alive after dark.

Reluctantly, Long Ridge got down from his horse. As he hit the ground, Matt said, very softly, "I understand, Chief. You don't have to prove your bravery to us."

Long Ridge smiled at the older Ramsey, feeling a little better. He nodded.

Matt hurriedly unsaddled Long Ridge's horse and then the black mustang. Buck had already done the same for Biscuit and Red Bird's horse.

"Unload that mule, please, Miss Red Bird," Matt said.

She did it quickly.

While the woman worked, Matt said, "Buck, give Long Ridge

his guns and fixin's. He'll help out, I reckon."

"What about me?" Red Bird asked, grunting as she dropped the sack of food onto the ground next to a tree.

"Ma'am?" Matt asked.

"I can shoot, too, you know," Red Bird said, a spark of the old defiance leaping into her eyes. She had straightened up and stood with her arms akimbo.

"I reckon you can." He thought a moment, then nodded. "Long gun or short?"

"Long, I reckon."

Matt nodded. "Damn long guns," he muttered. He handed her his rifle. "Mind you take care of it now, ma'am," he said.

"I will."

"Company's here," Buck called.

Matt turned and ran to a tree. He peered out past the trunk and the screen of brush and bare brown branches beyond. Red Bird moved to a spot between him and Buck, while Long Ridge took a place to Matt's left.

"That's them," Matt announced.

"Here, Matt," Buck called, "before it's too late." He leaned over and tossed his own Colt pistol to his brother.

Matt nodded. He was far more comfortable with a handgun than a rifle anyway, which was why he had given his Winchester to Red Bird. With two pistols, he would be deadly—once the outlaws got within close-enough range. Till then, Buck would have to hold them off with the Winchester.

"Don't none of you fire, less'n I say so," Matt ordered. "'Cept you, Buck. I'd suggest you take down a few of those bastards soon's they're in range."

"I'd already thought of that," Buck said with annoyance. His brother didn't need to tell him that. Especially in front of Red Bird.

"Miss Red Bird," Matt said quietly, "keep that Winchester handy. I'm figurin' Buck can fend them boys off and keep 'em from gettin' too close. But to do that, he'll need a loaded gun. He runs out, trade rifles with him and reload for him."

Red Bird's face darkened with a glimmer of anger. But she said nothing. She knew what kind of shot with a rifle Buck was, and she knew the wisdom of such a decision. It didn't mean she had to like it, though.

A jumble of fourteen riders suddenly popped up out of one of the numerous hollows in the land. This was the closest one, being about two hundred yards from the four's refuge. The fourteen trotted, seemingly unaware that death awaited them along the Arkansas River.

"Which one's Cross, Miss Red Bird?" Buck asked.

"I can't tell from here," she said, fear gripping her innards. Just the sight of this ravaging horde sent ice through her veins, as flashes of her subjugation and degradation by those men blurred her vision.

"No matter," Buck said. "I just wanted to shoot him first. But I'll just scratch whoever comes into my sights." He sounded more jaunty than he felt. He never liked killing, but he would not have any remorse about taking care of any of these men. Not with what they had done to Red Bird. He could just see her being ravaged by those leering, drunken animals, and . . .

Anger colored his face as he brought the rifle up. "I'll show you bastards," he mumbled under his breath as he aimed at a rider. He could see nothing of the man's features at this distance. But he wore a dirty duster and a soiled gray Stetson. He fired, and the man lurched, jerking upward before falling slowly off the back of his horse.

"Good shot, Buck," Matt said. He would not have any remorse about killing any or all the men in this frightful horde either. They were among the worst riffraff that ever rode through this land.

Buck paid his brother no heed. He simply levered another round into the chamber and fired. A second rider fell, and confusion broke out. Buck fired smoothly and steadily, and the horde turned and raced back to the gully. Another one of them died in the race, though, brought down by Buck's accurate fire.

"You don't mind if we was to go take a nap, do you, Buck?" said Matt, joking. "You can hold things down here while we do."

"Your snorin' would throw my aim off." He felt good, getting in a jab at his brother. Red Bird would not want a man who snored, he figured.

Matt pretended not to hear the remark, but he stewed silently.

"You think I should try makin' a run for it now, Matt?" Long Ridge asked.

"Still too dangerous. We can't see what those boys are up to. They might just be sittin' in the hollow, thinkin'. Then again, they might be ridin' down it one way or another, thinkin' to come up on us from another way."

"You figure to wait 'em out?"

"It's about all we can do, Chief."

CHAPTER
★ 24 ★

"I expect Cross'll wait for dark and send a few of his boys down here to test our mettle," Matt said. "We'll have to keep a close watch through the night."

"I expected so." Buck did not look at his brother; he kept his eyes scanning the horizon straight ahead and to each side as far as he could see past the brush and trees. Birds had begun chirping again, now that the antics of these unfeathered creatures had ceased.

They stood and waited, watching. After an hour, Buck said, "I expect things'll be quiet for a spell, Matt. But it'll be dark before long. We ought to have some grub."

Matt nodded. "Miss Red Bird, if you would please see to it."

Red Bird thought to refuse but then remembered she was still some miles from home. She would need the help of the Ramseys awhile longer yet. She forced a smile on her face. Resting Matt's Winchester against a bush next to Buck, she headed back toward the supplies, casting about for wood as she walked.

"I reckon you can go rest a spell while we're waitin', Chief," Matt said.

Long Ridge was too tired and dispirited to argue. He nodded. Carrying his old Starr rifle, he went back to their gear. Spreading out his blankets, he lay down, resting his head on his saddle. Within minutes he was snoring.

Matt and Buck took turns eating. Buck went to the fire first, grateful for its warmth. He ate slowly, trying to build up his strength for what lay ahead. He also enjoyed the few minutes it gave him to sit with Grace Red Bird, and the two chatted amiably. Buck knew Matt was watching them on occasion, but he didn't care.

Then it was Matt's turn to eat and try to impress Red Bird with his talk and stories. And it was Buck's chance to scowl at his brother and the Cherokee girl in between sweeps of the countryside.

There was no action for the rest of the afternoon, and Long Ridge slept on. Every few minutes, Matt or Buck would walk around a bit, stretching his legs and trying to get his blood moving against the cold that crept up from the river.

Darkness descended slowly, and with it came a slow, chilly drizzle. The Ramseys stood together, scowling at each other, their situation, and the foul weather.

"I don't expect 'em till after midnight," Matt said. "I figure they'll want to give us time to either fall asleep or get bored. But just in case, we'd best keep circlin' the camp, instead of standin' around."

Buck nodded, though Matt could barely see it. "What about them?" Buck asked, pointing at the Cherokees. Red Bird had, as the drizzle started, set a blanket gently over her great-grandfather's face. It was folded in such a way as to make a small tent, giving the old man breathing room. She was sitting with her back against a tree trunk, protected from the rain by the tree's bare branches and from the cold by the blanket she had wrapped around her. Her head dropped down toward her chest as she dozed.

"I think it's best they stay where they are. We put 'em in the bushes, they could get killed easy without us knowin' about it. They get too close to the fire, and they'll be easy targets. This way they're spread out, not so easy to take."

Buck nodded. "Want some coffee?" he asked. He realized he had been thinking poorly of his brother for some time now, and that bothered him. The offer was a small way to try to make up for that.

Matt felt much the same, and he nodded. "That'd be nice." As Buck turned away, he said, "Buck, I . . ." He stopped as Buck looked at him. "Ah, hell, never mind," he grumbled.

Buck got two mugs and filled them from the pot Red Bird had left on a rock in the fading fire to stay hot. They stood silent in the dark drizzle, sipping the steaming coffee. Both felt a tumble of feelings inside, a need to say something to his brother. But neither could bring himself to say what was on his mind.

"Well," Matt said, finishing his drink, "we'd better start movin'." He gave Buck his pistol back.

"Yeah."

They headed into the dark, walking slowly in a circle around the perimeter of their clearing. Buck carried his Winchester, not because he thought he would really use it in a night attack but because its familiarity comforted him. He carried it in his left hand, since he knew that if an attack came out of the night, it would be close in-fighting, and he wanted his right hand free to grab the Colt under his slicker.

Buck did not know how many hours later it was when he heard the sound. It helped that the drizzle had stopped a little while before. Despite his fatigue, he was still alert, and he stopped, listening intently for the sound. He nodded when he heard the scrape of canvas on wood. He knelt, figuring to present the smallest area to be reflected in the dim glow of the fire's embers.

He heard another sound and knew there were at least two men out in the brush, creeping up on their camp. He worried that there might be more. Suppose, he wondered, all of them were coming?

He eased out the .36-caliber Colt but held it inside his slicker, against his chest, to make sure it stayed dry. He watched intently, trying to see something, anything, in the Stygian gloom. He could not, but he was finally rewarded by hearing a branch moving.

Buck wondered when to make a move when he heard the loud bang of Matt's Colt. "Damn!" Buck mumbled. He shoved himself up, pulling his pistol out of his coat and firing all at the same time. He heard a shout of pain and knew he had hit someone.

He leaped to the side, landing with a splat in the cold mud. He slid around and pushed up onto one knee. A gun fired, and he heard the bullet slap into the mud behind where he had been a moment ago. He fired at the muzzle flash he had seen and was rewarded with another howl.

On the other side of the camp, Matt had also heard something faintly and stopped to listen. He heard it again, moving a little away from him, and he crept forward. He wasn't quite sure how he knew it, but he just suddenly became aware that someone was right behind the snoring John Long Ridge. Matt snapped his Colt up and fired. He knew instinctively he had hit his target—the faintly shimmering glob of the man's forehead.

He dropped to his knees as someone fired from the bushes behind and to his right. The bullet sent his hat flying. Matt did not even spin; he just cranked his body hard around at the waist and fired twice. He heard a grunt and then a body falling through brush.

He had also heard firing from where Buck should have been. As silence fell—except for the sound of people running through the foliage—he called, "Buck? You all right?" He was deeply worried about his brother.

"Muddier'n a wet hen, but all right," Buck said, a touch of annoyance in his voice.

Dawn was beginning to lighten the sky a little as Long Ridge stood up, rubbing his face. He looked depressed. Immediately upon awakening, he took in what was happening, and he was bothered that he had been snuck up on and that he had been able to do nothing to help the Ramseys.

Red Bird was up and moving, too, seemingly unconcerned. "Will it cause trouble if I build the fire up?" She shivered, still holding the damp blanket around her.

"Reckon not," Matt said tightly. He stood, pistol still in hand, turning in a small circle, listening, looking. The mist—or maybe just low-hanging clouds—was heavy, refracting the dim grayish light, making it hard to see anything more than a few feet away.

Red Bird shook off the blanket and tossed it aside. She grabbed wood from under a small tarp, where it would stay dry, and set about stoking the fire up.

"We best check on our pals out there, Buck," Matt said.

Buck nodded and edged into the thicket. He found bloodstains on the bare branches of a bush and followed the stains in the mud and on foliage until it opened out onto the plain. He could see only a few yards because of the mist, but he figured at least one of the two men he had shot had made it back to his friends. With a sigh, he turned back and fought his way through the clinging shrubbery. The other man he had shot was dead. He nodded, feeling no remorse, and headed back to the camp.

Matt knew the one behind Long Ridge's saddle was dead, so he went to check on the other. That one was dead, too, lying hung up on a thick thorn bush. He and Buck exchanged information over a cup of powerful black coffee.

Red Bird handed out plates of food, and they began eating. "What're we gonna do with those bodies, Matt?" Buck asked.

"They bother you?" Matt asked, his voice a little condescending.

Buck's hackles rose. "You know better than that, Matt. But they'll attract all kinds of scavengers. And unless they freeze up, they'll be high smellin' in a couple days—if we're still here." His voice let it be known that he was absolutely certain that if he were here in a few days, he would still be alive.

"What should we do with 'em?" Matt asked, almost sneering. "You want to ride up to Cross and hand 'em over?"

Buck was angry. There was no call for his brother to speak to him that way. He felt it a challenge to his manhood. "I think we ought to just toss 'em in the river," he said angrily.

Matt blinked and realized again that Buck was no frightened boy. He was a man, even if he did have a little filling out to do. "Sounds good," he allowed, feeling just a bit contrite. But not too much.

After their breakfast, Buck and Matt dragged the bodies down to the Arkansas under the watchful eyes of Grace Red Bird. The Ramseys tumbled the bodies into the water. The corpses bobbed along on the current until they disappeared around a bend.

"I don't suppose, Miss Red Bird," Matt asked as they walked swiftly back up to the camp, "that one of them was Harlan Cross?"

"Nope."

"What's Cross look like? Me and Buck never saw him. It'd be nice to know what the head man looks like. We get a chance to rub him out, we might set these other boys runnin'."

"He's a big man, near your size, Matt. But he's got a belly on him. He might be good-lookin'," she added with a shudder of disgust, "if it weren't for the eyes. They're flat, dead eyes. Brown. They never seem to see anything, but they do. They're creepy." She shut her eyes, as if to blot out the thought. "He's got a big scar down the left cheek, too," she said finally. She shrugged, deflated, and headed to where her great-grandfather sat by the fire. The old man coughed, and he seemed to be sickly, as well as tired.

"Why don't you get some rest, Matt," Buck said, thinking once again of the hard time Red Bird must have had. "I'll keep a lookout."

Matt was too tired to argue. He went and spread out his blankets.

The four people kept watch throughout that day, Buck and Matt alternating sleeping and watching. Nothing moved on the prairie, and by nightfall, Buck was hopeful that the outlaws had had enough and fled.

"Don't count on it, Buck," Matt growled. He was still tired. The catnaps he and his brother were taking were not enough to fend off exhaustion, especially when accompanied by the stress of waiting.

The Ramseys watched through the night, too, circling the camp again, but nothing came at them. The next day, though, shouted taunts floated down from the little rise above the gully. The outlaws hollered and yelled and occasionally set up a fusillade. The firing drove Buck, Matt, Long Ridge, and Red Bird behind trees, where they tried to watch, peering cautiously around the trunks. Bullets whizzed by, snapping branches and thudding into trees.

"Send out the girl and we'll let the rest of you go!" a voice came from afar.

"Do they really think we're that goddamn foolish, Buck?" Matt said, shaking his head. He didn't really expect an answer.

"Somethin's got to be done, Matt," Buck said, late in the afternoon. "We ain't had much sleep," he griped, "and we're startin' to run low on food."

"I been thinkin' the same." Matt sighed. "I reckon you or I ought to head for the fort. Try'n get help."

"What about Long Ridge?"

Matt looked over to where Long Ridge rested against a saddle. "He'd never make it, Buck."

Buck nodded. He had known it all along.

"What about me?" Red Bird asked.

"Too much could happen to a woman between here and there," Matt said roughly. He would not want to admit in front of Buck that he didn't want to let her out of his sight, especially if there was danger.

All of them except Long Ridge dove for cover when another burst of gunfire came from the outlaws' position. They waited it out and then gathered at the fire again.

"I still think I should go," Red Bird said.

"No," Matt said. "Besides, even if you got through, the army ain't gonna listen to a Cherokee woman complainin' about a bunch of outlaws comin' for her."

Her face tightened with anger and defiance. "Then send me out there to those bastards." Tears threatened, but she would not let them come.

BAD BLOOD

Matt almost choked on his coffee.

"What they're really after is me," Red Bird argued. "You give me to them, and they'll most likely let the rest of you go."

"No!" Buck said sharply, his eyes wild.

Matt said nothing, but looked askance at his brother. For the first time, he realized the depth of Buck's caring for Red Bird. It surprised him.

Red Bird grinned, but it was not a pleasant sight. She shook her head. "I know you two are fond of me," she said slowly. "But you best know, the feelin's ain't mutual."

"What?" Buck blurted, stunned.

"Oh, I like you both, I guess. You're fine gentlemen and all that. But . . ." She chewed her lower lip. She hated to do this but could see no way out of it. "I was leadin' you on. Both of you."

Buck's guts wrenched up into a knot. He wanted to cry, to scream and kick and shout. But that would be unmanly, so he sat still while his insides coiled with the sickly sour knowledge of betrayal.

Matt was furious. He was older than Buck and had seen far more of life's deceptions, big and little. It was part of the reason he was so angry. He should have seen this deception. He was also enraged that Red Bird would do this to his brother, tease him and lead him on in such a way. Matt figured he was man enough to withstand the pain, but he was not so sure about Buck. Not twice within three months.

"Why?" Buck managed to ask.

"I wanted to make sure me and Grandfather got back to our village. To do that, I needed your help. I figured the best way to get your help was to . . ." She trailed off, shrugging.

The Ramsey brothers looked at each other, their emotions mixed. Both wanted to hit the other or to comfort him. But they could do neither.

CHAPTER
★ 25 ★

Grace Red Bird was gone. And so were her horse and saddle. The Ramsey brothers looked at each other, accusation in their eyes.

"You were supposed to be on watch, Buck," Matt snapped, his irritation showing. His face was a mass of stubble, and his eyes were bloodshot from lack of sleep.

Buck looked little better. "So were you," he said heatedly.

They glared at each other awhile longer. Neither had heard anything, and that was embarrassing to them. They should have heard the woman getting her horse, moving away through the brush, and even entering the water. If she went north.

"You don't think she went *that* way, do you, Matt?" Buck asked, a chill twisting deep in his guts. He pointed to where the outlaws were.

"Christ, I hope not. How about it, Chief? She go and give herself to Cross to try to save our hides?"

Long Ridge shrugged. He was looking better. The several days of tension had affected him little. He had spent most of the time eating and resting and had improved from only two days before.

Matt was angry, disgusted, and confused. He sighed, blowing out his breath heavily and hoping it would carry away the feeling of festering uselessness that sat like a tightening band around his heart. "Best get breakfast goin', Buck," he ordered.

"You do it."

"What?" Matt asked, taken aback.

"You heard me. I'm sick and tired of takin' orders from you." He was, too. He had shown on the trip out that he could handle himself and any situation that came up. He had led four women, two boys, and two reluctant cowboys through Indian- and outlaw-infested lands. Granted, some of them did not make it, but that was mostly their own fault. Along the way he had fought Comanches, outlaws, and the elements. He had saved Matt's life. He had nothing more to prove to anyone. And just because he was the younger man no longer meant he had to do all the dirty work around camp, he reasoned.

The two Ramseys squared off, ready to knock the stuffing out of each other for the sake of pride. Or, more rightly, hurt pride. Neither was willing to admit that the Cherokee girl had affected him deeply. Nor were they willing to accept the fact that they had been played for fools by a sixteen-year-old woman.

"I'm of no humor for such shit, Buck," Matt snapped.

Buck shrugged. "You're hungry, you make some food. I ain't noticed your arms are broken."

Long Ridge stopped Matt's retort. "I'll make the food, damn-it." He knelt down to build up the fire. "But I'd suggest you two save your anger for those bastards out there."

Buck and Matt continued to glare at each other. Buck finally decided, though, that there was no shame in making the first concession. "I reckon Long Ridge's right, Matt," he said, with a measured dose of contriteness. His eyes remained fixed on his brother's.

"I suppose," Matt allowed reluctantly. He paused. "But once this is over, I'm gonna take after you for your insolence, boy."

Buck grinned tightly. "I whomped your ass good once already. I reckon I can do it again." He threw his shoulders back.

"Don't wager a lot on that, Buck," Matt snarled. "You seemed to've lost your respect for your betters."

"*Elders*, maybe. *Betters*, I reckon not." He shifted, looking beyond the trees to the ridge. "You got to remember, Matt," he said softly, "that I ain't the little boy you used to order around. I've proved myself enough."

Matt knew Buck was right; he had known it for a long time. But he was of no mood to admit it publicly now.

Further discourse was broken off when a splattering of bullets tore through the trees. Buck and Matt threw themselves down onto the cold ground, waiting out the fusillade.

When it ended and the Ramseys were getting up, a hollow voice floated to them from far away: "Your time's comin', Ramseys! Same for them damn Cherokees!"

Buck and Matt glanced at each other. "Reckon Red Bird's not with them, then," Buck said, grinning humorlessly. He turned and headed for the bushes that looked out over the prairie.

"Reckon not. Maybe she's made it to her village," Matt said, trotting alongside him. "She'll be safe there."

"You hear me, Ramseys?" the voice came.

"That you, Cross?" Matt bellowed.

"It is. You hear my warnin'?"

"You see him, Buck?" Matt asked.

"Just his hat. He's lyin' down, just pokin' his head over the edge of that little ridge out there."

"Why don't you give him a little greetin'."

That was one order Buck didn't mind taking from his brother. He raised the Winchester and aimed at the hat, adjusting for the distance and the breeze.

"You hear me?" Cross roared.

Buck fired. The bullet kicked up dirt just in front of the hat. "Damn it!" Buck snapped, unhappy about having missed.

"It shut him up, Buck," Matt said. "That's good enough. For now."

Long Ridge brought up two plates of food. He handed one to Matt, then walked over to give the other to Buck. "You boys ain't civil enough to set to eat together," he said sarcastically. "So you can stand there and eat while you watch for the bad guys to come and scalp us or somethin'."

Both Ramseys scowled at the old man, who walked away, chuckling.

"You know, Matt, the old coot's got a point. We have been a mite testy with each other of late."

"I suppose," Matt grunted. As long as he didn't think about Red Bird—and what she had done to him and his brother—he was all right. But as soon as he brought it to mind, his insides tightened up with shame, and he tried to deflect the self-loathing that cropped up onto others, particularly Buck.

They ate quietly and drank the coffee Long Ridge brought up after a bit. "We got about enough food for a day, maybe two, if we watch it," Long Ridge said, as he gathered up the empty plates and cups.

The Ramseys looked at each other. Matt finally nodded. "We'll sit it out today and take off either tonight or tomorrow."

"Across the river?" Buck asked, sounding a little disappointed.

"Or maybe that way," Matt said, pointing to where the outlaws were.

Buck grinned.

The day passed in cold, dull monotony, broken only by the sporadic bursts of gunfire from the outlaws' camp, or an occasional warning from Harlan Cross.

"What in hell are they waitin' for?" Buck groused just after the Ramseys' camp was sprayed by bullets again just after noon.

Matt shrugged. It did not require an answer.

Late in the afternoon, the Ramseys saw movement out there. Harlan Cross was standing behind a horse. "Your time's up, boys. Retribution is comin'."

Suddenly a line of almost two dozen riders formed along the horizon, all mounted and armed to the teeth.

"So that's why he's been stallin'," Matt said with a nod. It all made sense now. "He was waitin' for reinforcements."

Buck checked his Winchester. Matt did the same with his rifle, which Red Bird had left behind when she fled. Long Ridge moved up, his old Starr carbine in hand, his Texas Dance holstered at his hip. He took a position behind a tree to Matt's left.

"Takin' out the first wave's mostly going to be up to you, Buck," Matt rasped. He was tired, and he felt dull from it. His chest from the old wound no longer hurt, but some of the doubts that had accompanied that wound began to crop up again.

"I know."

"Here they come," Long Ridge said.

The outlaws flowed down toward the thicket like a heavy wind through a wheatfield. Buck braced himself, sucked in a breath, and began firing.

Between the dullness of the day and the pall of gunsmoke that soon covered the field of battle, it was hard to see anything after the first few minutes. Buck knew he had gotten at least two of the charging men, but he was not sure if they were dead or just wounded.

He heard Matt's rifle popping amid the hectic firing from the outlaws. Tree branches and pieces of bushes flew all about, and the roar from the guns was deafening.

Buck quit firing for a moment, letting the blue cloud dissipate in the breeze. The outlaws were close, but they could not breach the wall of thorn bushes. They turned and raced back up the slight incline and over into the gully beyond.

"Everybody all right?" Matt asked. His confidence was back. He had no more doubts about himself—or his brother. They were a team, the way it should be. When he got affirmatives from the two others, he shouted, "Reload. They'll be back."

The outlaws began moving into sight again, skylined on the snowflake-flecked horizon. Then came the seemingly slow-motion charge.

Suddenly Buck heard something behind him. "What the hell!" he muttered, spinning. Fear flashed through him. Had some of the outlaws gotten behind them? But he could see nothing through the brown thicket.

He spun back toward the front and began firing, trying to keep an ear open for whatever—or whoever—it was behind him.

The sounds behind him grew louder. He turned, the frigid fingers of fear grasping at his stomach and heart. Bullets roared through the leafless foliage, thunking into trees and whining off rocks. "Matt! Behind us!" he bellowed over the din.

Matt had heard the new noise, too, and had the same fears and doubts as Buck. He swung, figuring that if they were being attacked from behind, it would be close-in fighting, and he'd be best able to handle it with his Colt. He hoped Buck would keep his attentions toward the front, using the Winchester as effectively as he usually did.

"Good Christ!" Matt muttered in amazement.

He counted eighteen Cherokees, led by Grace Red Bird, shoving into their camp and sliding off their horses, dripping wet after crossing the river. The Indians—virtually all dressed in white men's pants, shirts, and hats, though with moccasins and war-paint—charged up to the trees and bushes near Buck, Matt, and Long Ridge. They began firing a dismal collection of old rifles and muskets. Only two of the men had new repeaters.

But the sudden boost in firepower caught the outlaws by surprise. They turned and tried to flee, but a withering fire from the thicket cut them down. Buck saw Garrick O'Fallon fall from his horse and lay still. His gray derby bounded and rolled away, and it was stomped into the earth by a running horse.

A moment later, Matt yelled, "There's Cross! Get him, Buck!"

Buck spotted Harlan Cross and smiled grimly as he aimed. He fired and noted with satisfaction that the bulky outlaw went down and did not move.

Grabbing their horses, the Cherokees raced out of the thicket and chased, howling, after the outlaws who were still alive.

Buck turned and leaned against the trunk of the tree, breathing heavily. Tiredness covered him like a cloak made of iron. His head fell onto his chest. He shook off the feeling a little as Matt came tromping up, whooping and bellowing a Rebel yell.

"Goddamn!" Matt roared. "Goddamn, we showed those bastards!" he howled again.

"Reckon we did," Buck said wearily. He shoved away from the tree. His legs feeling like lead weights, he moved toward the fire. His arm burned from the Kiowa-inflicted wound.

"Let me help you, Buck," a wildly grinning Red Bird said, hurrying to his side. She was near rapturous in her joy.

Matt felt a pang of loss, and of guilt, when he saw it.

But Buck shook the woman off. "Leave me be," he growled.

Red Bird stepped back, her eyes wide in surprise.

"You've caused me enough hurt," Buck said, a little more contritely. He made it to the fire and sat down. Matt joined him, as did Long Ridge, and then a suddenly tentative Red Bird.

"Thank you, Miss Red Bird," Matt said, trying to sound gallant but not all that pleased with the Cherokee right at the moment. "I expect we owe you our lives."

She shrugged. "It was nothing."

"How'd you manage it?"

She grinned viciously at her great-grandfather. "You might not have shamed them when you came after me, Grandfather. But you left the warriors feeling uncomfortable about letting you go off alone. They were sure by now that you were dead, but you were not forgotten.

"When I rode into camp, it was like they'd seen a ghost." She laughed. "It took some talkin', but I finally convinced them that if they didn't follow me back here, they would not be men; that there was some question about their manhood already for letting me be taken and you ride out by yourself. That did the trick, especially since some of the women took my side and began jeerin' their men."

She laughed again, and Matt realized it was the first time he had ever heard her laugh—really laugh. It was a pleasant sound, though a bit raspy and masculine for his taste.

"Well, we're obliged, Miss Red Bird," Matt said, emphasizing it, though it hurt him to say it.

"It was the least I could do," she said, casting her eyes down.

"Especially after what I did to you and Buck."

Matt grinned ruefully. "I should've known about it, but . . ." He nodded at Buck, who sat with his eyes downward.

Red Bird looked at Buck. "I know you don't think much of me right now, Buck," she said softly. She smiled wanly when he looked at her.

His face was etched with pain. First Eula Mae McFarrin, he thought, now Grace Red Bird. Life was cruel sometimes.

"But I did what I had to," Red Bird said. "My responsibility was to Grandfather. He had come for me, had helped me. I had to see that he got home. Can you understand?" she asked, a pleading in her eyes.

"I can understand," Buck said, his voice sounding old and far away. "But you didn't have to toy with us, play me and Matt off against each other." He breathed with a rattling sound. "All you had to do was ask us. We would've helped."

Red Bird's smile froze on her face. So wrapped up had she been in trying to keep the men interested in her—for her vanity, as well as for their help—that she had not been able to see that Matt and Buck were men of their word. They would have helped; they had offered to do so even after she and Long Ridge had stolen their horses. It would have been so simple.

"It hurts that you did that," Buck said. "Me and Matt almost come to blows over you." He shook his head, wondering how he could have been so stupid; how he could have been deceived so easily; how he could have thought so poorly of his brother. "Damn." He looked at Matt. "I'm sorry, Matt," he said sincerely, "for some of the things I said to you."

"Not half as sorry as I am, boy," Matt grumbled. He would get over this much more easily than Buck. For Matt, his attraction for Red Bird had been only an infatuation, though he had to admit he had lost sight of that for a while. But to Buck, it was something deeper and more important.

Red Bird was crying, and she realized it was for real. The pain she had caused these two fine men cut her deeply, and she regretted it. "I don't deserve even to have you both as friends," she said between sobs.

Buck looked at Red Bird and felt heartbroken. His affection for her still ran deep, though he knew she would never be his. After what she had done, he would not want her anyway. But that did not lessen his hurting any. He shoved himself up, shaking his head to try to clear the cobwebs.

"It's time we were on the trail, Matt," he said. "Miss Red Bird is with her people now and will be safe."

Matt worried about Buck. The younger Ramsey was paining inside because of this, and Matt hoped his brother would be all right. He stood up.

"But you've been up for days, almost constantly," Red Bird blurted, surprised. "You need rest, food."

"We'll make do," Matt answered. He clapped a big hand on Buck's shoulder. He grinned at his brother and winked.

Buck grinned back ever so slightly.

But when Buck did that, Matt knew his brother would be just fine. It would take time, but Buck would weather this. The Ramseys headed for their saddles.

SONS OF TEXAS

The exciting saga of America's Lone Star state!

TOM EARLY

Texas, 1816. A golden land of opportunity for anyone who dared to stake a claim in its destiny...and its dangers...

__	SONS OF TEXAS	0-425-11474-0/$3.95
__	SONS OF TEXAS #2: THE RAIDERS	0-425-11874-6/$3.95
__	SONS OF TEXAS #3: THE REBELS	0-425-12215-8/$3.95

Look for each new book in the series!

Check book(s). Fill out coupon. Send to:

BERKLEY PUBLISHING GROUP
390 Murray Hill Pkwy., Dept. B
East Rutherford, NJ 07073

NAME_____

ADDRESS_____

CITY_____

STATE_____ZIP_____

PLEASE ALLOW 6 WEEKS FOR DELIVERY.
PRICES ARE SUBJECT TO CHANGE
WITHOUT NOTICE.

POSTAGE AND HANDLING:
$1.00 for one book, 25¢ for each additional. Do not exceed $3.50.

BOOK TOTAL	$____
POSTAGE & HANDLING	$____
APPLICABLE SALES TAX (CA, NJ, NY, PA)	$____
TOTAL AMOUNT DUE	$____

PAYABLE IN US FUNDS.
(No cash orders accepted.)

203b

A special offer for people who enjoy reading the best Westerns published today. If you enjoyed this book, subscribe now and get...

TWO FREE

A $5.90 VALUE—NO OBLIGATION

If you enjoyed this book and would like to read more of the very best Westerns being published today, you'll want to subscribe to True Value's Western Home Subscription Service. If you enjoyed the book you just read and want more of the most exciting, adventurous, action packed Westerns, subscribe now.

Each month the editors of True Value will select the 6 very best Westerns from America's leading publishers for special readers like you. You'll be able to preview these new titles as soon as they are published, FREE for ten days with no obligation.

TWO FREE BOOKS

When you subscribe, we'll send you your first month's shipment of the newest and best 6 Westerns for you to preview. With your first shipment, two of these books will be yours as our introductory gift to you absolutely FREE, regardless of what you decide to do. If you like them, as much as we think you will, keep all six books but pay for just 4 at the low subscriber rate of just $2.45 each. If you decide to return them, keep 2 of the titles as our gift. No obligation.

Special Subscriber Savings

When you become a True Value subscriber you'll save money several ways. First, all regular monthly selections will be billed at the low subscriber price of just $2.45 each. That's